I0534194

Aunt Anne's Archive

Tales of Magic and Mystery

By Deby Fredericks

Aunt Anne's Archive

Dedication

For the two women writers who have inspired me:

Anne McCaffrey
Tanith Lee

Indicia

Text © 2024 by Deborah J. Fredericks.
Cover illustration by DeKreator. Design by Deby Fredericks using Canva. All rights reserved.

No generative AI has been used in the conceptualization, development, or drafting of this work.

No part of this book may be reproduced in any form or by any electronic or mechanical means, including information storage and retrieval systems, without written permission from the author, except for the use of brief quotations in a book review.

This is a work of fiction. All characters and events portrayed in this book are fictitious, and any resemblance to real people is purely coincidental.

Also by Deby Fredericks

Minstrels of Skaythe Series
The Tower in the Mist
Dancer in the Grove of Ghosts
The Ice Witch of Fang Marsh
The Renegade of Opshar
Prisoners of the Wailing Tower
The Tale of the Drakanox

Novels
The Seven Exalted Orders
The Grimhold Wolf
Too Many Princes
The Magister's Mask
The Necromancer's Bones

Novellas and Novelettes
The Weight of Their Souls
The Gelboar

Also by Lucy D. Ford

Aunt Ursula's Atlas
Masters of Air & Fire

Acknowledgments

"The Atlantis Appeal" was originally published in Lorelei Signal Magazine, (July, 2017)

"Bonewood Forest" was originally published in Andromeda Spaceways Inflight Magazine, #25 (2006)

"The Elfin Cow" was originally published in the anthology, *Well, It's Your Cow*, by Impulsive Walrus.

"Good Old Vernon" was originally published in Lorelei Signal Magazine, (April, 2017)

"Hoard" was originally published in the anthology, *The Dragon's Hoard*. Originally published by Sky Warrior Books, it is currently available from Wolfsinger Publishing.

"Lord Harrel" was originally published by PESFA, the Palouse Empire Science Fiction Association, in the early 2000s. Unfortunately, I have lost the publication and do not have a specific date.

Table of Contents

Bonewood Forest

Hazel Farseer strode onto her front porch. She wiped her hands on her apron and frowned. Hazel was a big woman, her broad face weathered with cares. The farm where she lived was serene and safe, but the Bonewood Forest lay just across the Fleetwater River. That was too close for her liking, though the trees kept to their side of the water all right.

She watched them anyway, day after day. Especially on days like this, when her husband was away and her only company was their son, a youth of sixteen years. Hazel did not trust those trees, with their twisted trunks white as bone and their leaves dark as dead flesh. The Bonewood Forest filled the western horizon with its gloom. Not a bird or beast lived there, not a nut or berry grew. Only vapors, dank and foul, moved among the deathly ranks of the trees.

Because she watched, she saw the stranger appear. A lone man, covered in a dull blue cloak, led a black and white cow with a small cart hitched behind it. Now, who in the world would use a dairy cow for hauling?

Hazel watched with her lips pinched together. On this side of the river, pastures dotted with cattle slanted down toward the water. The hills behind the house were green with cabbages, turnips, and the vivid green of young rye. The stranger followed a bend in the river, making for the ford where shallow waters slipped over gravel bars. No one had used that ford since... How long? Since Owen Makefire went into Amberdale for supplies. And that was months ago. No one else came out of Wakedell that spring. If they had, Hazel would have seen them pass.

She didn't like it, not with Alder away, but she had bread to knead and clothing to mend. Hazel went into the farm house and back to work, but a part of her was alert, listening. She did not trust anything that came from the Bonewood Forest.

When the dog started barking, she dropped her knitting and strode to the door. She came out on the wide veranda in time to see Briar emerge from the stable, where he had been working. The stranger had turned into their yard -- but it was no man. A maid of perhaps seventeen approached. Her young face wore a queer, set expression that was far too mature for her years. The black and tan hound skidded to a stop in front of her, roaring and snarling in his fury.

"Heel!" Briar called as he ran forward. "Lion, heel!"

The dog obeyed, growling, but the maid ignored both of them and led her cart right up to Hazel's doorstep. The cow was terribly thin, her udders shrunken, and the girl looked little better.

"Here now!" Hazel barked herself, when the stranger came a bit too close. "Who do you think you are, just coming onto my land like that?"

The maid stopped at last, and regarded Hazel with

2

weary eyes. "I've come seeking shelter," said she, in a toneless voice. "I'll work, if you let me stay."

Briar came to stand beside his mam, with Lion at his heels. They both looked the stranger over. The maid was too thin to be pretty. The hood of her cloak covered hair the color of dried straw, and her skin was brown from working outdoors. Her skirt and bodice were mis-matched, both garments threadbare and patched. The white of her blouse bore dark stains.

Hazel snorted, a quick rebuff on her lips, but then she stopped. The maid's eyes were blue, paler and more piercing than the sky. Hazel had seen such eyes before.

"Who are you?" she demanded. "What were you doing in the Bonewood Forest?"

"I am Rowan Makefire," the maid answered, as if that explained everything.

In a way, it did. "Makefire — Willow's daughter?"

Willow Silverweave had been Hazel's dearest friend, until she married Owen Makefire. The Makefires lived in Wakedell, right up against the Bonewood Forest.

"Aye." Rowan's voice was flat. "But Mam is dead these three years."

"I'd heard that," Hazel said. Strangely, she felt better that the maid did not pretend otherwise. "Then where is your father?"

"He went into the forest."

Rowan said no more. Hazel stood solid, but inside

she shuddered. The only time she ever set foot in the Bonewood Forest was for Willow's wedding. She could never forget the pale trees crowding up beside the road, and the hissing among the branches even when no wind blew. Fallen leaves swirled across the road, even in spring, and off the path they lay so thick it smelled as if something had died. Hazel missed Willow, and thought of her often, but no friendship was enough to make her set foot on the bank beyond the Fleetwater again.

And now came Willow's daughter, so haggard and worn, begging shelter.

"Mam? You know her?" Briar asked. Hazel had forgotten he was there.

"I knew her mam," she told him. And to the maid, "You can stay. I'll make it right with my man when he gets home."

Rowan merely nodded. Her tense face showed no pleasure or relief. "I'll put my cow in your pasture, then, and let her graze."

"It's over here," Briar said eagerly, though Lion remained hostile and alert. "I'll show you."

The offer met no enthusiasm. "If you want," Rowan said. With few movements she unhitched the cow and let the tow bars fall into the dust of the farm yard.

"What's wrong with your cow?" Briar asked as they walked away. Just like him, to worry over a sickly animal.

"Fear," Rowan told him in a dull, flat tone. "She'll get better, now she's away from the trees."

4

The two youngsters walked off, with the sullen Lion slinking after them. Briar looked at Rowan with alarm, but Hazel heard no more of what they said. She lifted the canvas cover from the cart, revealing the few meager things Rowan carried with her from Wakedell. But with that movement a heavy odor of decay came up into Hazel's face. The smell of the Bonewood Forest, and no mistake. She caught a breath between her teeth and wondered if she was doing right.

She went into the farm house, to cover that stench with the warm scent of baking bread. There were sleeping arrangements to think of, as well. Hazel had no daughters for Rowan to share a room with. It was not for lack of trying. Eight little darlings rested under the sod on the hill above the farm, and four of those were girlchildren. Briar was the only survivor of all she birthed. And it came to Hazel that, just perhaps, Rowan Makefire might need a mother's comfort as much as Hazel longed to give it.

Hazel had just begun shifting materials from her sewing room when Briar returned. He was a gangly boy, still growing into his height, with dark hair that curled like Hazel's and bright brown eyes like his pop's. His fair and open face was pinched with worry.

"Where is her pop, Mam? She won't tell me."

Every dark tale Hazel had ever heard crowded her mind. It was said the trees of that forest walked on their own, that they sang songs to beguile the unwary. They had razors for leaves and their roots drank of human blood. Wakedell had been a goodly town once, but the passing years sapped its life. Folk there must ride over to

5

Amberdale to see a blacksmith or a barber. It seemed to her ominous, now, that Owen Makefire was the only one to stir from Wakedell this year. And Rowan said even he was gone.

"How many times have I told you, boy?" Hazel snapped. "That place is cursed. If Owen Makefire went in there, he's dead."

What youth ever listened to his mam? Briar stared at her, disbelieving. Then he caught his breath. "Then she's lost her mam and pop both? That's too bad."

The lad's sympathy for Rowan's plight spoke well of him, but Hazel cautioned, "Let her be. She'll tell you about it when she's ready. Now go on and get Rowan's things from her cart. Then put it beside the barn."

Because Briar was a good lad, he did as he was told. After him came Rowan. "I noticed your turnips need weeding," she said. "I'll start on that, if you want."

"You don't want something to eat?" Hazel asked. Thin as the girl was, she ought to be hungry.

Rowan shrugged. There was no change in her still face. The blue eyes were closed up like shutters in a storm.

Now Hazel must take her own advice, and wait until Rowan was ready to talk. "The turnips can wait," she said. "We'll prepare this room for you to sleep in. You can help me with that, if you're not tired."

There was a flicker behind those eyes then, some emotion she did not want Hazel to see. Then Rowan nodded. Silent as a ghost, she went to work.

Not long after, Alder Farseer came home for his nooning. He heard the tale of Rowan's arrival from Hazel and Briar together. Alder was a rough-looking man, one with the stones he'd used to build his farm house. For all his hard seeming, his beasts knew the gentleness of his hands. Alder never argued what Hazel was set on.

"You know what's best," was all he said. He kissed Hazel's cheek and sat down to eat.

Days passed by, and Rowan Makefire remained a puzzle to the family. She wanted no mothering, that one. No girlish confidences, no sewing pretty things. From sunrise to sunset, the hardest work on the farm was what she sought. Rowan carried water, swilled out the hog pens, washed the laundry, hoed the vegetable fields. Days turned into weeks. Her gauntness filled out and she became a lovely maid. Yet not for a moment did she pause in her work. She seldom spoke, never smiled.

Hazel's house had not been so clean in years, nor her fields so well tended. And never had her son been so distracted. Briar was as merry as a summer's morn. He lived to make folk smile, especially the maidens, like Rowan. But, Hazel thought, there were times when the boy wasn't very bright. Everywhere Rowan went Briar followed, wanting to help her or playing little tunes on a wooden pipe. But always her shoulder was to him, her face turned away. It drove the boy half mad.

Alder thought it was funny. "Back up, boy," he chuckled. "Women don't like to be crowded."

Hazel thought it was sad. She kept a close watch on

7

the two of them, just the same. When Rowan seemed ill at ease, Hazel sent her son to chop firewood. He did it with a will.

Even so, the maid's silence tore at Hazel's heart. It wasn't right that a child of Rowan's age should bear such grief by herself. If she had been a hired girl, a stranger, Hazel might have let it pass. But this was Willow's daughter, practically blood kin. She could not turn away.

At least once each day, Hazel found some reason for Rowan to stay inside, with her. Usually it was work in the kitchen, where the great hearth warmed the house. While they plucked a chicken or pieced together a quilt for Rowan's bed, Hazel reminisced about the days when she and Willow were young.

"One time," she said, "on All Fools Day, Willow and me played a trick on our big brothers. We wrote them love notes and invited them to a tryst, but when they got there, they were trysting with each other. How we laughed at them!"

Or she told Rowan, "Your Mam made the best pastries in town. The bidding would always go high when she sold at market."

Silence was Rowan's only reply. She seemed to have no interest in events before her birth. Her wary glances said she understood what Hazel was trying to do and she wanted none of it. Ofttimes, between her chores, Rowan stood at the pasture fence and stared westward toward the murky expanse of the Bonewood Forest. It filled Hazel's heart with despair to see this, for what did her little farm have to offer against the grim power of the forest? Still, her life had taught her patience. She could only keep trying, for Willow's sake and her own.

One morning, the two women worked together in the kitchen. Rowan churned butter while Hazel chopped meat for the stew pot. She worked at a wooden counter, its smooth face seamed with scars from many years of such work. At one end was a deep sink, half-full of water. Copper pots, agleam from Rowan's polishing, hung from pegs above her. A sturdy wooden table was loaded with turnips and carrots for the stew. The kitchen door stood open, admitting soft breezes to cool the stuffy house.

Hazel carried the meat by handfuls and placed it in a fire-blackened cauldron on the hearth. She added a few measures of water from the barrel beside the door and swung the heavy pot into the hearth. Then she filled her apron with vegetables and put them in the sink to wash. Hazel had run out of stories to tell, and she had no more heart to listen to herself blabbering. She had thought to let Rowan work outside, alone, but Briar had been after her to look for wild plums with him. Hazel knew she had to spare the girl.

It was this matter that finally broke the silence in the kitchen. Hazel sighed as she began peeling the turnips.

"About my Briar," she began. "Is he troubling you?"

"He's all right." Rowan bent over her churn, raising the plunger and ramming it down. The muffled gurgles of the churn seemed to fill the kitchen with sound that had no meaning.

9

"He means well," Hazel sighed, "but he doesn't have much sense."

"He doesn't understand," Rowan said.

Hazel hesitated, and told her, "I'm not sure I understand,"

"You do understand. I've seen the way you watch the forest." The maid's lips twitched in what might have been a smile. "And the way you watch me. You are true to your name, Hazel Farseer."

That made Hazel pause, looking at her strange charge. Rowan worked now, as she always did, with fierce energy but no joy.

"You watch the trees, too," Hazel ventured. "What is it you seek?"

"I just watch," Rowan said. "Gram always did, same as you do. She told me once you must let the trees know you're watching, else they think they can do as they please."

Rowan paused in her work, tilting the churn to feel if the butter was solid inside. She raised the plunger again and added, "I don't know if I believe it. I mean, that a wicked thing can be kept in check just by showing you know it for what it is."

Coming from Rowan, this was a deep personal revelation. Hazel turned the words over in her mind, savoring the precious moment. If only the subject of this confidence was not so ugly. It must have been the summer sun, so hot outside the farm house, that made Hazel feel prickles of sweat along her spine.

10

Lowering her voice, she asked, "What did your Gram tell you about the trees?"

Rowan fell silent, her face taking on a familiar, shadowed look. In the stillness they both heard footsteps. Heart jumping, Hazel turned to see Briar stride in. His cheeks were flushed and his brows bent with anger. Rowan quickly went back to work, as if the noise of her churning might block out the intruder.

"You answer my mam," Briar ordered. His stern face looked like a stranger's, not the clever and smiling lad Hazel knew. "We've fed you and sheltered you, Rowan Makefire. You owe us the truth."

"Briar!" Hazel said, hot with embarrassment, now, that he heard them talking about him. "Who taught you manners, boy?"

Her son ignored her, seeing only the maid before him. His voice trembled with earnest. "Day after day you look at those trees, but you never look at us. Why?"

You never look at me, he meant. Briar spoke with the agony of a lover denied, and Hazel's heart went out to him.

"Briar," she repeated, softly now. "Be still."

Once again Rowan stopped working. She held to the plunger with white knuckles and leaned over the butter churn like a crutch.

"Understand me, Briar Farseer." Her eyes were the brilliant blue of dying flames. "Everyone I love is dead. I will never love again, not until this is done."

11

"How can you say that?" Briar choked.

"You said you wanted the truth," Rowan answered.

The boy's face was ruddy, and his hands worked at his sides as if he wanted badly to hit someone. Maybe he did, after seeing his hopes shattered, and in front of his mam, too.

"Briar." Hazel moved to embrace him. "Son."

Briar jerked away from her. In a strangled voice he said, "I'm going to go chop wood."

He slammed out into the yard. Hazel was left standing with a lump in her throat. She was accustomed to Rowan keeping a distance, but Briar's rejection burned like the fire on the hearth.

Then came the sucking and swishing of the butter churn, and Rowan's voice, too steady and calm. "You've been good to me, Hazel Farseer. I wouldn't take your boy from you."

Perhaps that was meant to be comforting. Hazel drew a long breath, as if she must remember how to breathe. Outside, she could hear Briar's axe working just as hard as Rowan's butter churn.

'Not until this is over,' Rowan said. And, 'I wouldn't take your boy.' Hazel couldn't understand what Rowan meant, or maybe didn't want to understand, but fear drove into her heart with every stroke of Briar's axe. She swept her chopped turnips into the stew pot and went in search of her husband.

When he heard her account, Alder sighed. "Best he learns it now, if the answer is no."

But the passing days became painfully awkward. No more did Briar whistle and smile. He working at his chores with a kind of hate. Hazel had nothing to say to Rowan any more, for she knew the maid would not hesitate to reject her just as she had Briar. Mealtimes were worst, with a blanket of silence over the table like an early snow. Talk of the coming harvest, or that Rowan's cow gave good milk these days, could not cover the rift. Such matters were irrelevant to Briar's grief and Rowan's closed heart.

Though the days seemed long, the year was swiftly waning toward fall. Harvest time came, and the family worked from dawn to dusk bringing in the rye, turnips and cabbages. Hard labor gave them all a measure of peace, for a tired body must sleep soundly. But the question hung over them, in the dust and chaff, how a divided family could endure the long dark of winter.

Soon the winds of autumn came, hissing through the stubble fields like unseen serpents. The gusts rattled the shutters, and Hazel woke in the night wondering who was trying to get in. Then she heard something else. She sat up in bed, listening. That was Briar's voice. No, Briar and Rowan.

The night air felt very cold as Hazel got out of bed. She wrapped a robe over her woolen nightgown and woke Alder. Together they hurried over chilly stones toward the sound of voices. A faint, flickering light told them a candle was lit in the kitchen.

Briar's accusing voice came louder as they drew near. "You are going away. I knew it."

"It's my duty," came Rowan's reply, as flat and unfeeling as the first day she arrived.

Hazel felt her heart tighten. She strode into the kitchen angry. "See here, you two. It's still dark outside. What are you doing up yet?"

A single candle burned in a cup on the table. Its lonely flame sent shadows flickering in the dark cavern of the nighted kitchen.

Briar turned with a guilty start when his Mam spoke. Then he straightened defiantly. "Ask her." He jerked his thumb at Rowan, who faced him across the supper table.

The maid glanced toward the door, where Alder and Hazel stood. Her face was still and intense. A leather rucksack lay open on the table before her, holding shapes of bread, cheese and sausage wrapped in coarse cloth. She turned with an angry jerk and went to the hearth, where she sat down stiff-backed.

Like Alder, Briar was in his nightshirt, barefoot beneath it, but Rowan was dressed for travel. She wore a sturdy blouse and bodice, winter leggings under her skirt, and the heavy boots Hazel had given her for working in the stables. Over all was her frayed cloak, covering her with the gloom of the Bonewood Forest.

"Well?" Briar demanded. "Am I wrong, or are you going off without so much as a fare-thee-well."

14

Alder said, "Son, we'd like to hear what she has to say."

Hazel waited, her hands clasped painfully tight. Life on a farm wasn't easy, and she had learned to face the many disappointments without fear. But somehow this daughter, who was not her daughter, filled her with pain. She hoped against hope that Briar was wrong. Hope was all she had.

But it was not enough. Rowan bowed her head. "He is right. It is time for me to leave."

"Child, no!" cried Hazel. "Are you so unhappy here?"

"I have brought only trouble to your house," Rowan said, as if that excused anything. "Now the winds have begun. That is all I was waiting for."

All these months, she had only been waiting her chance to leave them. Hazel tried to put her own pain aside and think of Rowan. "But why? You've escaped the trees of the Bonewood Forest once. Why must you dare their power again?"

"What power?" Briar burst out, half-laughing and half furious. "They are trees! Nothing but trees."

"Something wicked lives among those trees." Hazel's life-long fear sounded foolish, when she said it out loud. She hurried on, "It is a hating, hungry thing. Rowan, you can't go back there."

"I must," the maid answered, with a trace of sadness. "I have faced the forest before. It will not take me unawares. But others may not be so careful. I will not allow anyone else to suffer as I have."

Briar set his hands on his hips, determined not to understand, but Alder said, "I've heard many rumors. Can you tell me what gives the forest so black a name?"

"I will." Rowan sounded resigned that her escape had been foiled. Still she did not look at her hosts, and her voice became brittle and tense. "In olden times, my Gram told me, the trees could walk about and speak. Their long lives made them arrogant, and their numbers made them fearless. They looked upon humans as no more than food, and they hated our axes and our fire. So in every town there was a witch, and one of her duties was to make the trees behave.

"But in these days we do not credit the old tales. We think of the trees as having no understanding, nor do we believe in witches. Now it is humans who are reckless and proud. It was the foolishness of Wakedell that brought this upon us."

As she spoke, Rowan took up a small shovel and jabbed at the ashes of the fire with angry strokes. A few bright sparks flared in the shadowed cave of the hearth.

"And what is the power of these trees, that makes them so terrible?" asked Briar, scornfully.

"Their songs," Rowan answered. "Songs filled with false images and dreams to lure the unwary. Whatever you love, or lust for, or desperately need, they sing and make it seem real. But then there are branches that strangle, or leaves sharp as knives, or deep bogs to suck you down. And the trees have their feast."

16

She spoke of these things with an eerie calm and Hazel, remembering the sinister whisper of the leaves, swallowed heavily. Even Briar shifted restlessly in his place. Rowan spread a kerchief on the hearth, and placed upon it a small clay pot. She removed the lid. The shovel moved again, turning over a chunk of wood from last night's fire.

It was Alder who broke the silence, in his slow, calm way. "Did such things happen in Wakedell?"

Rowan nodded, not speaking.

Briar stared at her, the way he had when he first learned she had lost her parents. "Why was it allowed?"

The maid shrugged. "Different folk have different ways. My Gram, she came from Marshward, on the west of the Bonewood Forest. Only there, they called it the Whispertrees Wood. Whenever the trees started talking, their witch would set fire to the forest.

"But in Wakedell they held the woods as sacred. Burning was forbidden. If someone was lost, they said it was his own wickedness that brought him down. When the trees started talking, they held a town meeting. The men drew lots. Whoever got the mark, they chose one of their beasts, a cow or a pig, and left it in the woods. They thought if they fed the trees it would satisfy them."

There was no disguising the bitterness in Rowan's voice. "You know what happens when you feed a beast. It grows, and it wants more food. After a while, Gran said, they were having their meetings every month. Then every week. Nobody had any animals to spare, and still the trees

17

whispered and lured."

Rowan drew a shovelful of coals from the fireplace. She watched them burn steadily, then tilted the shovel over her pot. Orange sparks flared as the embers fell into the pot and vanished. One of these went astray and tumbled to the floor. Casually, coldly, Rowan set her foot down and ground it out.

The maid went on, "Gram had come to Wakedell as a young bride. The elders would not hear her warning, for she was a woman and an outlander. But at the end, they stopped having meetings. The folk couldn't face each other. Then neighbor fell on neighbor. They seized each other's children from the streets and dragged them screaming into the woods. But those who took them vanished, too."

Hazel stared, transfixed by her cool description of a community's disintegration. "How did they stop it?" she asked.

"They didn't." As she spoke, Rowan took a few twigs from the kindling box. With brittle snaps, she broke them up and added them to her firepot. "The trees were sated at last. For all the years of my pop's life, they slept. But Wakedell could not survive. The families who still lived did not trust each other, and what is a village without the trust of neighbors? Many left. They were the wisest. All who lingered are dead."

Except for Rowan, of course. Hazel understood now why she hardened herself, with such a dreadful burden to bear.

"How is it the trees took your loved ones?" Alder

18

asked. "You said they were asleep."

"No longer." Rowan placed the lid on the pot and knotted the four corners of the kerchief with fierce jerks. "As a child, I remember seeing birds and small animals in the woods, but that changed when Mam died. It was an accident, but it seemed her dying woke the trees all the same. The beasts and birds began to vanish, and Gram heard the trees singing. Pop went to warn the neighbors, but they set their dogs on him at Smithiron Farm. I guess they'd already lost kin, and feared we would turn on them. We kept to ourselves after that, trying to keep our beasts away from the trees.

"Then Gram died at the end of last winter. She coughed and coughed, and couldn't stop. I went to the Plowfield's, to ask Gram Plowfield over for my Gram's wake, but the farm was deserted. I saw only dogs and chickens gone wild, and not many of those. It was the same at the Crosswater's and the Smithiron's. In town the buildings were deserted, with trees growing out the windows and pushing down the walls. They were too big to have grown so quickly. They must have walked," Rowan said with grim certainty.

"Pop had already plowed our fields and put in seed, and we couldn't afford to give up the crop, but it was hard going. We both heard the trees calling with Mam's voice. That was hard for Pop to bear. I stayed with him, talking over the sound of the singing, but one morning I couldn't find him. He must have gone into the woods during the night.

"I kept things up as best I could by myself, hoping

he might come back, but he didn't." Rowan's voice as numb and flat, as it had been when she first came to the farm. "The trees sang all the time. I heard Pop's voice, and Mam's, and even Gram's. I heard music and laughing in the leaves, wolves howling and babes crying, and more. I'd only the cow left for company. It was driving me mad. So I fled then, and came to you here."

Rowan sat terribly still, staring into the feeble coals of the fire. A long silence stretched out, flexing like a branch drawn tight enough to break.

"Why would you ever want to go back there?" Briar asked with horror.

And Hazel, who never begged, said, "Rowan, child. I knew your mam so well, but she went with her husband into that awful place and I never saw her again. For her sake, let me help you. Don't go."

Rowan shook her head slowly. "When I left the Bonewood Forest, I thought I would run far away and never return. But I cannot do that. The trees are already moving. Soon they will make for Amberdale."

Alder made a hiss in his teeth, and Hazel bit her lip. She had dreaded those trees all her life, and yet it came as a shock to think they might cross the river, invade her sheltered home. Yet the water ran low now, after the hot summer. Only the drama unfolding in Hazel's kitchen kept her from running to her front porch and making sure the trees were still on their own side of the water.

"What can you do?" Alder asked.

20

"These woods have been too long without a witch." Rowan spoke with cold ferocity. "The trees will teach me how, but first I must tame them."

"But how?" Hazel pleaded. "You said yourself, their numbers are endless."

Rowan Makefire smiled, a grim stretching of lips that brought no light to her eyes. "Those who worshiped the forest are gone now. I want to try Gram's way."

Hazel caught her breath sharply. Rowan had just said she was waiting for the winds to blow — winds that could whip a small blaze into an inferno that even the ancient trees must fear. Rowan was not returning merely to join her family in death. She intended to exact her vengeance, and perhaps keep the evil in check.

"Let me come with you," Briar said suddenly, understanding it, too. "I've been cutting so much wood, I can do it all day without tiring."

"No!" cried Hazel and Alder together.

"You cannot help me." Rowan sounded hard-hearted enough to be a witch, even without the trees.

"You shouldn't go alone, if that place is what you say it is," Briar argued. "Not asking for help is what killed your neighbors, just as much as the trees did."

"Listen to your mam, boy." Alder began, but Briar exploded.

"I'm not a boy!" he shouted. His fists clenched as if he would strike at the older man. "I'm going!"

21

"You are staying here," Alder repeated. Hazel had heard him use that tone before, when he was cheated in the Amberdale market or if someone impugned the quality of his cattle. Never before to his own son.

Rowan straightened, lifting her firepot by the knotted kerchief. She rounded the table and slapped Briar across his face.

"Day after day you followed me and stared at me," she said, "but it was never for love of me. It was because of what you wanted for yourself."

Briar staggered backward, raising a hand to the red mark on his cheek. Only Rowan seemed calm, wrapped in her purpose like another cloak. But this one held back warmth and kept her heart cold.

"Today you will think of someone besides yourself," the maid went on. "You will consider your parents, who might lose their only child to the Bonewood Forest. You will stay here."

Rowan turned away, while Briar was still stunned by her words. And Alder stepped up, laying his arm about the boy's shoulder. To comfort him, or maybe to hold him back. Rowan placed her firepot into the rucksack. She held her cloak aside to shrug the leather straps over her shoulder.

The door opened, showing an icy pale dawn sky. Gusting wind seemed to fill the kitchen, cold as the air under the trees. It tore at their night clothes and the pots on the walls made a low keening.

"I won't forget what you've done for me," Rowan's voice came back among the wind's shouting. "If I can, I will return. I promise that."

Then the door closed, and Rowan was gone. Briar took a step forward, and Alder's fingers dug into his shoulder. But it was Hazel who stopped him. She caught her boy about his chest and hugged him. This time he did not resist.

"Let her go now," she said urgently. "She said she'll come back. Take this time to think what you want from her, and why you want it."

Briar nodded, rubbing at the lurid mark on his face. It broke Hazel's heart to see him look so defeated.

That morning passed in desolate silence. There was much work to be done yet, but Alder stayed close to the house, watching in case Briar tried to slip away. Hazel stayed in the kitchen, alone. She had worked so for many a year, but never before felt so lonely. Autumn winds buffeted the solid stone farm house, and Hazel tried to console herself that Rowan Makefire had such a powerful friend to help her. Yet fire and wind were treacherous allies. She feared Rowan's plan would mean the end of her.

Before nooning, Briar called to Hazel suddenly. He and Alder stood at the fence, just where Rowan used to stand and watch the forest. The hills about the farm were dry and brown, aged by the summer's passing, but no longer was the western horizon black with trees. Billows of smoke rose above the forest, turning the sky gray as a dirty sheet. Rowan Makefire had been true to her name.

23

That burning went on for many days. At night the west glowed a sullen orange, as if the sun was about to rise from its grave. Briar spent long hours at the fence, watching the smoke shape itself into tapestries of destruction. He played his flute and the wind carried his music away, though maybe not far enough for Rowan to hear.

Ofttimes Hazel stood with him. She did not watch the sky, but the ford across the Fleetwater River where Rowan had first appeared. It seemed impossible the maid could do as she said, tame the forest and seize its power for herself. And yet, Hazel believed Rowan would succeed. The Bonewood Forest would have a witch again, to make the trees behave themselves.

And then, who could say? Even a witch needed warm lodgings for the winter. Maybe, at last, Hazel would have a daughter of her own. So she hoped, she and Briar together, that love would be stronger than the curse of the trees.

Household Chores

"Honey!" Phostan's voice floated down the stairs. "Have you seen my Blood-Stone medallion?"

Rhella of Silverdale straightened from adding wood to the kitchen stove. She tossed her long, red-brown hair over her shoulder in an exasperated gesture. As if she didn't have enough to do already...

"Where did you last have it?" she called, striving for a patient tone.

"Never mind, I found it."

Phostan of Silverdale strode into the tidy kitchen, fastening a brilliant red stone around his neck with a golden chain.

Rhella frowned as she took in his splendid Mage-Militia uniform: the blood-red satin cloak, the helm with its proud cockade, the breastplate etched with protective runes. Phostan's wand was in his hand, long and silver and with another Blood-Stone in its pommel.

"Where are you going?" Rhella asked.

"I have a challenge today," Phostan said airily. "Didn't I tell you?"

"A battle?" Dismay shone in Rhella's gray eyes.

"Don't worry, it's just a practice match against Albercrom."

Phostan spoke with exaggerated kindness, as if Rhella was a child. She hated when he did that. It wasn't as if she didn't know what he was talking about. Her own parents had both served in the Mage-Militia for their home town. Rhella herself had trained with the local Youth Battalion.

"Honey," Rhella protested. Phostan strolled on into the parlor. Rhella left her cooking and followed him. "The roof still leaks where the Giant Eagle landed on it, and the foundation is cracked from that Shock-Wave attack. You promised to fix them."

"I know, sweetheart, and I will. But I can't ignore a challenge. I've been building my rank for both of us. You should understand that," Phostan said petulantly.

What Rhella understood was that her husband cared more about these trivial battles than he did about his responsibilities at home. No Umbrian had dared the borders of Gastornia in nearly a century. The Mage-Militia was little more than an elite men's club, play-fighting for their own amusement. Rhella closed her mouth to keep from saying something she would regret later.

Noting her silence, Phostan rolled his eyes upward and kissed her briefly. She did not respond.

"I'll get to it later," he said. "I have to go. Albercrom is waiting."

Rhella glared at him. "Don't teleport in the house!"

she warned, a moment too late.

Fuming, Rhella opened the windows to clear the noisome vapors from the air. Then she stalked back into the kitchen to stir the stew pot before it boiled over. Drat the man, always leaving when where was work to be done!

Well, Rhella had had enough. She tromped up the stairs to the bedroom and rummaged in her cedar chest. From its depths she extracted her own magic wand and medallion. In contrast to Phostan's gaudy Blood-Stones, Rhella used Sun-Stones, pale and strong as aged whisky. She stormed back down the stairs. Phostan wasn't the only one who knew how to manipulate *oespre* power. Rhella rolled up her sleeves and began to chant.

~ ~ ~

Phostan reappeared in front of the cottage. His shoulders were slumped, his armor was scuffed, and there was a pall of dust on his scarlet cloak.

"How did Albercrom do it?" Phostan lamented, although no one was listening. "There was no *oespre* power, and none of my Minions answered the summons! If not for my Blood-Stone, I'd..."

He started to slouch toward the door, but stopped as if Spell-Bound.

"Aaugh!" Phostan cried.

Standing beside the whitewashed cottage was Stumpy the Mastodon. His huge, hairy trunk unfolded lazily, raising a bale of hay up to the roof. A pair of Wing-Women received it. Near them, a veritable cloud of Silver

Sprites patched a series of long gashes in the thatched roof. Stumpy helped himself to a mouthful of hay before lifting another bale.

On the other side of the cottage, half a dozen Rock-Gnomes applied mortar to the building's foundation. Beyond a low stone wall, a Greenwood Elf was hoeing in the vegetable garden. Ogion the Bull-Man came around the corner from the wood pile, hefting a load of firewood. He brushed past Phostan and ducked through the kitchen door.

Except for Stumpy, all the Minions looked embarrassed, but that was nothing compared to how Phostan felt.

"Wha... Wha..." the Mage-Militiaman gasped.

"Ahem." Someone coughed politely behind him.

Phostan whirled to see Bezilband, his Infernal Attorney, standing on the porch steps. Bezilband wore a ruffled apron and rubber gloves over his dapper black robe. Through the open door, Phostan could see several Barbarian Warriors sweeping, dusting and washing windows with far more energy than skill.

"Bezilband!" Phostan shrieked. "What are you doing here? I called for you, and you didn't answer my summons."

"I'm terribly sorry, Master Phostan," the Attorney replied. "We had already been summoned by Mistress Rhella. According to the terms of our contract..."

"Summoned by Rhella?" Phostan interrupted. His cheeks slowly turned pink. "I lost the match because of this!"

"I see." Bezilband paused. "Er... can't you do something about this, Master Phostan? The Rock-Gnomes and the Mastodon don't mind, but I'm afraid Ogion is rather upset."

The Bull-Man snorted loudly as he emerged from the kitchen and headed for the wood pile.

"Yes, yes. Of course." Phostan snapped his fingers impatiently. "Go, all of you. Go."

The Minions stopped for a moment to look at Phostan. Then they continued with their chores.

"Master Phostan," Bezilband said, with another apologetic cough, "I'm afraid that, according to our contracts..."

"I know, I know," Phostan groaned. "Rhella summoned you, so she has to dismiss you. Where is she? I'll talk to her."

The gleam in his eye hinted at more than mere words.

"She went out on the Giant Eagle, sir," Bezilband said.

"Joy-riding, at a time like this? Oh, great. That's just wonderful."

"Yes, Master Phostan," Bezilband glumly agreed. "Well, if you'll excuse me, sir."

The Infernal Attorney picked up a bucket and mop

from beside the door and stepped back into the cottage.

~ ~ ~

Evening shadows grew long.

The Minions had completed their tasks. Unable to depart, they loitered in the yard all afternoon. The Barbarian Warriors sparred half-heartedly with Ogion. The Silver Sprites played aerial tag with the Wing-Women. Bezilband, the Greenwood Elf, and the Rock-Gnomes sat at the dining room table, throwing dice.

Phostan roamed the cottage disconsolately. His initial fury had long since cooled. Perhaps, he admitted to himself, Rhella did have reason to be angry. This was the first time he could remember anybody helping out with her chores. If she would only come home, he would try to make it up to her.

But more than that, he wondered what was for dinner. And how was he supposed to feed all these Minions, if Rhella stayed out late? Stumpy was reaching over the wall to tear branches from the neighbor's Golden Apple tree. Phostan was going to hear about that, he just knew it.

At last, he heard the rush of wings and the fierce cry of the Giant Eagle. As he rushed downstairs, he heard his wife's voice concisely dismiss the Mastodon, the Greenwood Elf, the Silver Sprites, the Bull-Man, and the Rock-Gnomes.

"Honey?" Phostan peered out cautiously. "I wanted to, uh..."

He opened the door just in time for the Barbarian Warriors and the Wing-Women to enter. Each carried a large bundle marked with the stamp of the Addis of Ababa. Rhella coolly dismissed the Wing-Women, the Barbarian Warriors, and the Giant Eagle. The Minions gratefully faded in billows of acrid vapor. Only Bezilband still lingered hopefully to one side.

"Ahem," he coughed politely.

Phostan felt his temper stir. He reminded himself that he was going to apologize to Rhella. And he had to admit that, for a woman who had caused her husband a major inconvenience — and probably spent a lot of money — she did not look especially happy.

"What were you saying?" Rhella turned to Phostan. Her gray eyes were sharp as daggers.

"Well, I was going to apologize for dueling Albercrom when you asked me not to. I, uh... I lost anyway. I'm sorry, and I won't do it again," Phostan finished in a rush.

The steely eyes softened a little. "Then I'm sorry I summoned all your Minions and used all the *oespre* power."

"Great!" Phostan said, much relieved. "Let's have dinner. I'm starving."

"Oh? I'm supposed to forgive you, just like that?" Rhella snapped. "And we can all to back to just the way it was?"

"I said I wouldn't do it again," Phostan answered

31

defensively. Then he saw that she was teasing.

"Well," Rhella smiled slyly, "I think we'd better discuss this with *my* Infernal Attorney."

Hoard

Strangers were camped at the ford. The dragon Carnisha slithered up to a rock ledge where her tawny scales blended in. Her tail lashed across dead needles under the scrub pines until she stilled it.

"Well, well," she growled.

As she watched with cold intensity, two menservants did chores. One cut firewood while the other swept out a fine brocaded tent. A well-dressed gentleman stood aside, contemplating the play of morning light on the River Lyre.

"Humans," Carnisha hissed. "They think whatever they see belongs to them."

Long ago, the mighty Cragmaw Mountains had been the dragons' kingdom. Until humans came over the sea and invaded. Other dragons had been killed or forced to retreat, but Carnisha would never give way. It seemed the seeds she had been sowing were bearing fruit at last.

Carnisha studied the gentleman, with his silken robes and pearly skin. A nobleman, she assumed. However, she had some suspicion about the servants. Sun-darkened and strong, they worked with little skill. Nor did their rough clothing match their master's finery. They had knives in their boots and sharp eyes glancing about. What nobleman would travel with such ruffians? Perhaps they were bodyguards.

The she-dragon eased back and circled down to the road. Before she left the trees, Carnisha hunched forward. She tucked leathern wings against her back and tail close to her ankles. Concentrating, she turned around slowly, drawing on the powers of sky and land to spin the change. Horny hide and glinting talons reshaped into a dingy dress and ragged hood. Gray hair wisped about a wizened human face.

Disgusting, but needful.

Gone was Carnisha, scourge of the mountains. An old woman stepped onto the road, bowed by the weight of a peddler's pack. Muddy clogs grated over gravel and dirt. She set off, humming a shrill drone so those ruffians would hear her coming and think themselves clever.

As she neared the ford, a man bellowed, "Hoy! Over here!"

A wide grin split her sagging face as she feigned surprise at seeing the camp.

"Hoy to you, young'un!" Carnisha waved, then tottered as if the pack would drag her to earth.

"Show courtesy to your elders, Robin," the nobleman chided. "Go help the poor woman."

Stone-faced, the man who had been cutting wood strode over the flat rocks that paved the ford. He grabbed her scrawny arm.

"What a kind young man," she beamed, as if he wasn't dragging her along. "Taking care of li'l ol' Nisha."

"Mum," Robin grumbled.

"Are you indeed the famous Nisha?" The nobleman fell in beside them, taking Robin's place. "Fetch us another chair, Nick, and see if there's tea to share."

"Famous, is it?" Carnisha cackled. "How would a grand lord such as yourself know of ol' Nisha?"

"No lord, alas. I am but a humble scholar," the gentleman corrected indulgently. "Edwin Frastian, at your service."

"I be Nisha o'th' Glade." Carnisha bobbed a curtsey. "Well met, good scholar."

"Well met, Nisha o'th' Glade," Frastian eagerly replied. "Recently, a friend of mine acquired a fascinating pendant from an antiques dealer. It was very old. I was truly envious."

"Ah," Carnisha smirked. "Was this an emerald pendant, or pearl?"

"Pearl, dear lady."

"Pearl, you say? That would be Berlack. What a nice young man. So glad he found a home for that trinket of mine."

"Indeed he did," Frastian agreed. "Upon inquiry, Berlack revealed that he had acquired the piece from a sweet old peddler woman at the ford of the River Lyre, near Mount Cragmaw. And here I am, ready to buy."

They reached the camp. Robin had built up the fire and Nick unfolded a wooden chair by the fireside. At the mention of emeralds and pearls, they both studied her with hungry eyes.

"Do sit, dear mother." Frastian helped Carnisha into the chair.

"Why, isn't this lovely?"

She let him fuss over her, knowing how anticipation would build. He doted, offering dried dates as well as tea, while the alleged menservants lingered nearby. After Carnisha had eaten and drunk, she bent to unflap the top of her peddler's pack.

"I sell only to a few, like Berlack," she prattled. "Those who have shown I can trust them. An old woman can't be too careful."

Nick coughed a little, and Robin elbowed him.

Frastian frowned, until she twinkled up at him. "Since you've been so kind, I suppose there's no harm."

"You flatter me." A narrow hand touched his chest with apparent modesty.

Carnisha started with a jumble of second-hand wares. Tunics of cotton cloth, only a little stained. A copper pot darkened by use. Wooden sandals with frayed straps. The scholar made interested noises, but kept trying to see into her pack.

At length she unrolled a felt bundle. "Not sure what these are, but I find 'em lying about. They do have a shine, eh?"

Oddly shaped flakes curved from the ground of drab felt. They were tawny brown, no two the same size, and might have been horn, though the glint spoke more of metal.

Frastian leaned forward, knuckles white over his chair arms.

"My dear Nisha, these are dragon scales!"

Carnisha knew that quite well, since she had shed them. She bobbed her head. "Dragon scales? You don't say."

Nick stepped closer. "T'would make a fine armor if you had more of 'em." Robin nodded wisely.

"Get back," Frastian snapped. "You're shadowing the wares." Nick gave his master a dark glance, but obeyed. Frastian picked up a scale.

"Careful, they're sharp," Carnisha warned.

"So they are." Frastian dropped the scale to suck on a fingertip. He explained, as if Carnisha was a child, "We know there once were dragons in this province, but they were wiped out long ago. The Cragmaws, here, were their last refuge." His other hand gestured to take in the rocky peaks looming beyond the river.

He sounded so pompous, Carnisha could hardly bear it. She brought out her finest baubles.

"Maybe that's why I found these."

The sword hilt was leather, cross-wrapped in a style long out of use. The blade had broken off a few inches down.

"Must've been a scrum," Robin observed.

"'Twould seem." Carnisha shrugged and brought out a silver goblet, now black with tarnish, and a small dog carved of jade. One amber eye had been picked out, leaving a socket full of dirt.

"These are rare treasures." Frastian breathed. He turned the goblet to see how badly the stem was bent. "This is done in the Beshanthine style, and the sword is from Old Aerde."

The menservants traded lustful glances over his head. Carnisha wondered that Frastian trusted them as much as he appeared to.

"Were these all together?" The scholar's voice shook, words tumbling over each other. "You may have found a dragon's lair. Think what I could learn if I studied the place where a dragon once dwelt!"

"Think of the hoard," Nick murmured to Robin.

Frastian scolded, "Don't be crude. Their value goes far beyond mere gold. Nisha, you must tell me where you found these pieces."

"'Tis my own secret!" She drew back, clutching her pack.

"Nay, dear Nisha," Frastian pleaded. "I am a scholar. I simply must study this location!"

This fervor was exactly what Carnisha needed. She reveled inside, while retorting, "Nay, sir. You could be robbers, after all." She stuffed the sword hilt back into her pack and reached for the jade statuette.

"Please, dear lady! These are not just trinkets, they are priceless relics. Each tells a tale from the distant past. And these are the most precious of all." Frastian gingerly touched a scale. "Allow me to make an offer. I insist!"

"What's your price, then?" She rolled the scales up in the felt, but not too quickly.

"A silver penny for each scale," he ventured, watching her carefully. "There are sixteen, if my count is correct. The other pieces are damaged, but I still may be able to learn from them. Say fifteen pence for the sword, four for the goblet, and..."

Priceless relics, he said? What a cheat. Carnisha's hands didn't falter.

"Berlack pays in gold."

"You over-estimate my resources," Frastian protested.

Carnisha cast a canny eye over his silken robes, the black hair pulled into a sleek top-knot, and the shimmering brocade of his private tent. She plucked the goblet from his fingers and tucked it into her pack.

"Wait," the scholar moaned.

Robin put in, "Now then, Mum. Money ent the only thing. How'd it be if we carried a load down for you? Nick and me, we're right strong."

"Less trips for those poor ol' legs," Nick wheedled.

"What are you saying?" Frastian objected.

Carnisha quavered, "You bounders, would you take an old woman's livelihood?"

"Nay, Mum. You've got it wrong," Robin coaxed. "Master Frastian here has enough to pay for all you've got."

"Or he can just buy the whole lair," Nick added.

Edwin Frastian gaped, horrified. Then he closed his mouth and slowly smiled.

"I'd need time to make arrangements, but then I could examine the lair thoroughly and record where the artifacts lie. Brilliant!"

"What a fairy tale." But Carnisha let them see her hesitate.

"Leave the hard work to us young'uns," Nick said. "You can get yourself a little farm or a cottage on the lake."

"Think of it," Rob urged, "living in a warm, dry house 'stead o' these cold mountains."

"Here now." Frastian seized control. "I'll gladly pay a fair price, but I simply must see the location beforehand."

"And if you don't like what you see? You'd still hold my secret," Carnisha whined.

"No need to worry," Frastian said. "If there's nothing to see, there's nothing to tell about."

Carnisha picked at the felt enclosing the scales. The three men watched her with hopeful dread. More than likely, the two servants would follow her anyway. She was tempted to let them do it, but then Frastian might escape with the warning.

"It does sound lovely," she said, tantalizing them.

"Excellent!" cried Frastian, while Robin and Nick playfully shoved each other in celebration.

~ ~ ~

Some hours later, Carnisha led her dupes up a steep slope, halfway to the summit of Mount Cragmaw. Every so often she pressed a hand to her side.

"Me ol' legs," she would say. Or, "What a hike."

The two servants were hale and hardy, easily keeping pace. However, the scholar struggled. Many hairs had come loose from his topknot and stuck to his pale, sweaty face.

"Surely we'll be there soon?" he puffed.

Before Carnisha could reply, Nick squinted ahead of them. "What's that?"

Gray-brown rocks loomed, mottled with lichen and moss. A crack angled between them, darkness lurking beyond.

Robin smiled. "Looks like a cave."

"A crag maw, indeed," Frastian chuckled as excitement overcame effort.

They all surged forward, bumping Carnisha. Robin and Nick shouldered each other in the gap.

"You men," Frastian scolded. "Let me see before you trample all over it."

They scowled, but let the scholar pass. When Carnisha arrived he was practically crawling over the cavern floor, like a bizarre toad emerging from spring mud. Holes and heaps of dirt pocked the surface. Only a little light flowed from the entrance. Frastian bent closer to brush at something.

"Another scale. Wonderful," he mused to himself. Nick and Robin edged by.

"Don't see any treasures," Robin muttered.

Nick whispered, "Hoy," and jerked his chin toward a further gap leading off the first chamber. "Think it goes through?"

Frastian was more alert than he seemed. He straightened in time to see the two men slip into the gap. He rushed after them, crying, "Don't touch anything!"

Carnisha sneezed as running feet kicked up dust. Already, exclamations echoed from the rocky passage.

"Worth a hike, I'd say," cried Nick, and Rob gloated, "Nick, lad, the gods must like us." All the while Frastian babbled, "A hoard, a real hoard. I hardly dared hope!"

Carnisha reached the opening. The two ruffians traded back-slaps while Frastian stood rapt. Rays of light from cracks in the ceiling revealed an untidy mound of gold and tarnished silver. Jewels glittered and the occasional shield or urn stuck out. Near the center, several pairs of bright blue eyes flicked open. As soon as they saw Carnisha they winked shut. Tawny scales blended perfectly with the hoard.

Frastian exulted, "Well, will you hear my offer?"

"Gladly, good master," she simpered.

As soon as Frastian's back was turned, Nick knelt beside the hoard. Grinning, he buried both hands above the elbow in clinking coins. Then he winced and jumped back.

"Hoy, something bit me!"

"Where?" Robin wrestled Nick's sleeve up, revealing an arc of four oozing punctures. He glared at the hoard.

Frastian, meanwhile, gave Carnisha a cunning eye. "A thousand should be a fair price."

Playing for time, she folded her arms and stared at him.

"Think of all the work to be done," he reasoned. "Men to hire, bribes to —"

Grimacing, Nick rubbed his arm. "Rob, help me! It burns!"

"Don't touch it." Rob began wrapping his belt

around Nick's arm above the bite.

"What are you two getting into?" Frastian demanded.

"Look you," Robin growled. "Nick's been bit."

"He shouldn't have touched anything. Trying to help himself, no doubt," Frastian answered suspiciously.

"What?" Nick stepped forward, still clutching his arm.

The three of them fell to disputing over who needed whose permission for what. While they argued, Carnisha turned around slowly. She straightened her neck and flexed her wings, grateful to regain her superior form.

At this signal, her brood rose among the hoard. Coins clinked and slithered off horny heads, long necks, low bodies plated with scales. Pale blue eyes blazed with glee. If the wings were too small for flight, the talons were sharp enough.

"What are those?" Rob shrieked. He kicked out, but the first of the brood sank its fangs through his trousers. "Get off me, you devil!"

"Gods, no!" Nick tried to run, but the venom had done its work. His knees crumpled. Two of the brood held him down as his body arched in spasms.

"Impossible," Frastian bleated. He turned to flee, but skidded to a halt as he saw Carnisha blocking the only way out.

"You want to know about dragons, little scholar?" She lowered her horny head to his eye level. "We are predators. The hoard is what we use to attract prey."

"No," he pleaded, looking around wildly. "You're supposed to be gone!"

"I never left. I adapted." Her head snaked forward, fangs piercing cloth and skin as she clamped about his middle. Frastian screamed and clawed at her eyes. She shook her head and held him until his struggles ceased.

Shrieks gave way to the rasp of scales as Carnisha's brood gathered. Wings flapped and excited tails swiped the floor.

"We did it," one of the males crowed.

"So sneaky, so sly," said a female.

Another said, "We hid as still as dead bones!"

"Can we eat now?" asked a different male.

"Watch," she commanded. "These colorful robes will be a fine addition to my peddler's pack."

The brood observed with shining eyes as she demonstrated how to remove clothes from a dead human without ripping them. And then, a good feast for the six dragonets.

"Eat well," she crooned, as her brood tore into still-warm flesh. "With this you will grow strong."

A bloody dragonet raised her head from Frastian's side. "Thank you, mother!"

"Soon we'll be big enough to earn our own names," a male bragged.

Carnisha regarded them without affection, for love meant nothing to her, but rather with fierce satisfaction. One day, she and her brood would drive those human intruders out of the Cragmaws, and they would rule their ancient kingdom once again.

Buried Treasure

"This project is completely ridiculous. You know that, don't you?" Miguel teased as he steered his hovercar along the disused highway west of Reminade.

"Yes." Eliana Alamilla chuckled, although the truth stung. "It's so ridiculous the dean didn't even bother to reject my proposal. That means I can do it, right?"

"As your loyal brother tags along." Miguel sighed with dramatic suffering.

"Because he's the best brother ever." Eliana batted her dark eyelashes.

"More like, my hovercar has enough room for your gear — Whoops!"

Eliana's shoulder bumped the passenger door as Miguel swerved around a four-foot-wide gash in the asphalt.

"Not much maintenance out here," he complained.

"This far from the city, there aren't enough people left to justify doing the work." That was the sad reality. Eliana drew a brown finger across her tablet's glass screen, adjusting the vintage map it displayed. "We're getting close, though."

"How can you tell?" Miguel waved at the landscape passing on either side.

Farm fields had been given back to nature decades ago. It was all prairie now. Fence lines were lost amid the wildflowers and waving grasses. Dark freckles broke the monotony — horses and cattle, set loose when no one was left to care for them.

"That's Coyote Willow up ahead," Eliana said. "Or what's left of it."

The road curved around a long ridge covered in sagebrush. The hovercar's thrumming shifted lower as Miguel dropped to a cautious pace. Vacant buildings rolled past — a bank, a florist, a gas station refitted into a coffee stand. Farther back, orderly rows of decaying houses with empty windows for eyes seemed to gaze on them wistfully.

In Eliana's screen, a tiny blue arrow crept across the antique map. As they left the derelict town behind, she murmured, "Look for a left turn. It'll be hard to spot after this long."

"Just part of the fun," her brother answered cheerfully. "Like a treasure hunt."

"Yeah," she chuckled. "Some treasure, though."

Route signs flitted past as they both scanned the overgrown roadside. Miguel slowed abruptly.

"Could that be it?"

There was a slight widening of the raddled paving, and a faint track of cracked asphalt between banks of weeds.

"Good eye." Eliana fist-bumped her brother's shoulder.

The narrow side road led off into the fields. Hoverblades flattened the flowers and grass as they followed it around another sage-grown hill. It emerged into a shallow valley where scrub trees overhung a rusted chain-link fence. A mound of tumbleweeds crowded against it.

"This has to be the place." Miguel guided the hovercar to a relatively level patch near the ramshackle gate.

"I think so, too." Eliana blanked her tablet's screen. While her brother set the vehicle down, she reached for her filter mask. A quick hand caught her dark curls into a ponytail, and she slipped the mask over it.

Tightening the straps, she imagined the smells of the countryside. Dust floating around the vehicle would be gritty and faintly sour. There would be a light sweetness of green life, too. Eliana would never know those smells herself. Born afflicted with GP-2 that severely impaired her lungs, she rarely tasted the outdoor air.

"Radio check." She thumbed the button under the mask's chin. "Check, check."

Miguel adjusted his headphones. "Loud and clear."

With gear in place, they both exited the cab. It was extremely quiet in the open country. Every wisp of wind sounded like a vent fan. Miguel made his way back, leaning slightly on the side of the car. The back hatch squeaked loudly as he raised it. Eliana lowered the tail gate with a crash. Equipment thudded and scraped as she organized it.

"Metal detector first?" Her brother's voice crackled in her ear.

"That's fine," Eliana said. "I'll turn over some dirt. Remember, we have to validate the site's age. As close to 1960 as possible, or it won't do any good."

"Don't worry so much," he bantered. "The project is ridiculous, remember?"

Walking with a tilt and a jerk, he went to the rusty gate. Instead of GP-2, Miguel had GP-5. A twisted back and crooked hip were facts of life for him. Bolt cutters snapped, and the corroded gate chain slithered down with a dissonant clank. Eliana frowned when the radio carried his slight grunt of pain.

"Don't push too hard, we've barely started."

"Ah, it's nothing," he answered with cheerful bravado. As if to prove it, he pushed the gate wider. Chain link squealed over asphalt rubble. "Wonder how long it's been since anyone opened this."

"At least a hundred years." Eliana hurried to catch up with him. "Coyote Willow closed their town dump in the late Sixties. That's why I hope we can find what we need here."

She slipped on heavy protective gloves before passing over Miguel's metal detector. Her disabilities weren't as visible as her brother's, but they were just as bad. Not only did GP-2 scar her lungs, GP-7 had cursed her with an immune deficiency. Digging through this old garbage dump was a real risk. Who knew what pathogens lurked among the buried refuse?

But what was that hazard compared to the thrill of their adventure? Eliana's heart skipped with excitement. Given her disabilities, it was no surprise she hardly ever got the chance to do field work. Besides, what if she was right? She would spend her hospital time in a haze of joy.

"Happy hunting." Miguel clapped Eliana's shoulder before he limped off, adjusting the length of the metal detector. Eliana brought a shovel and rake, with a bag of smaller tools rolled over her shoulder.

The siblings were hardly alone in their disabilities. After a century or more of relentless chemical exposure, humanity now suffered six major genetic plagues and nine minor ones, with others not even discovered yet. On top of whatever else they did, several of the plagues damaged human fertility.

Thus the emptying out of small towns around the globe. Every year, fewer babies were born. Of these, many suffered severe impairments. No one escaped the legacy of the toxic 20th century. That was why Eliana had to leave her office, with its safe, filtered air, and chase an absurd treasure.

She took a moment to scan the old dump site. You could see where the natural slope angled down, only to smooth out into artificially level ground. Miguel headed across the middle, step after labored step. The metal detector slowly swung back and forth before him. Eliana moved to her right, giving him space. She probed between clumps of grass with her shovel. The chuff-chuff of impact came muffled through her protective visor.

"I'm getting a lot of hits." Miguel's voice cracked over the radio. "How deep would you say they buried their trash?"

"Not very. If they were closing it, all they wanted was to keep the smell down. They didn't get fancy with capping and membranes for methane collection until almost the 21st Century."

"So, two feet?" Leaning slightly on the metal detector, Miguel turned and started back toward her.

"Not even that."

As Eliana spoke, her shovel point hit something. Carefully she scooped the dirt away. A large jug emerged. The label had long since deteriorated, but the orange plastic was as brightly colored as the day its long-ago owner tossed it aside. She tried to work her shovel underneath it, but it cracked into splinters.

She sighed to herself. "I'm not supposed to collect artifacts, anyway."

Miguel joined her in pacing off a ten-foot square. Together they dug through the upper layer of dirt and grass. Eliana's back and shoulders hurt. Her breath rasped inside her face mask, and sweat tickled where she couldn't itch it. But when they stopped to rest, they surveyed a lumpy surface where endless junk peeked out.

There was bright red, rusty metal. Unrecognizable rags of fabric and plastic. Glass bottles and crockery survived relatively intact. A few tougher pieces of food waste, such as corn cobs and bones, still kept their shape.

"We need to find a newspaper," Eliana said. "They printed it on actual paper back then, and it always had a date."

"Then I'll start looking for the real prize," came her brother's sarcastic reply.

They searched separately, each working their way along one side of the ten-foot square. Eliana's heart ached for the slapdash methods they had to use. As a historian, she wanted to examine the artifacts with respect before carefully cataloging and preserving them. The best she could do was capture images. There was no time for more, even if anyone was left to care about 20th Century history.

In fact, her partners at Reminade University were only interested in one kind of relic.

"Ugh, what is this?" Miguel straightened up, gagging.

"You know that's why I value your assistance, right?" Eliana teased. "A functioning olfactory system is crucial to this project."

"Bleah." He coughed a little more, shoveling loose earth over whatever created the offending odor before continuing his progress deeper into the garbage dump.

Eliana threw that thought away as her rake clawed up shreds of pale brown material. She knelt eagerly and fished a trowel out of her bag. With gloved hands, she extracted a bundle a long as her forearm from its earthen tomb.

"Yes! Here it is."

Miguel came over, leaning on his shovel. "Got something?"

Darkened paper was still tucked tightly around itself. With careful hands, Eliana flattened the newspaper and turned it right-side up. Though torn by the rake, it was still readable.

"County Gazzette," she read reverently. Bold letters on top read, FEDS TO SHUT ALCATRAZ. Skimming past that, Eliana found the finer printing beneath. "March 8th, 1963. We're in the right era!"

"Never doubted you, sister."

The two of them slapped their gloved hands in celebration. Then Eliana re-rolled the newspaper and slid it into a sterile fabric specimen bag. After all that had happened, nobody wanted to use plastic any more.

Now the serious digging began, hard work lightened by many smart remarks. "Here we have the ultimate in broken bar stools," Miguel quipped. "Ah, a perfect example of mid-20th Century, mass-produced dinnerware," Eliana replied in the tone of a stuffy professor. "With matching cutlery."

Even so, the afternoon dragged on. Excitement of

her discovery gave way to dull exhaustion. Breaks for water and rest became more frequent as Eliana insisted Miguel sit down to ease his back and hips. Focused on her own search, she almost didn't hear her brother's shout.

"Hey, look at this!" Miguel shook earth out of something. "It's a baby bottle. Broken, though." The glass was so dirty that it hardly reflected sunlight at all.

"Keep working in that area," Eliana croaked wearily. "Maybe you'll find what we're looking for."

And he did, almost immediately. Half a dozen rounded lumps were nestled in the torn shreds of a canvas garbage bag. Heart jumping, hardly daring to hope, Eliana worked one free.

"Gross," Miguel backed off a few steps. "My olfactory system confirms it."

"We have to be sure."

Eliana ran to fetch a steel tray from the hovercar. She placed the bundle into the tray. After checking her gloves for punctures or tears, she carefully peeled back the outer edge. Thin fabric, formerly white, tore loose from a layer of coarse pebble-like material.

"Is it supposed to look like that?"

"They used a gel to absorb moisture." Eliana spoke softly, concentrating, while she worked her trowel under the crusty material. It came up as a piece, and she gleefully examined the dark brown matter trapped beneath.

"Miguel, my brother, this is it!" Eliana hugged her

trowel and danced in a circle.

"I can tell." He waved his hand in front of his face, groaning and grinning at the same time. "I've heard that one man's trash is another man's treasure, but this is ridiculous."

"That is ironically appropriate." Eliana rolled their prize back up and slipped it into another specimen bag. "Let's take them all back to the university. The gene docs are going to go nuts."

Soon the hovercar lifted off with its priceless cargo. Once the cab was sealed, Eliana pulled her mask off. She ran her hands through sweat-dampened hair and savored the chance to breathe freely. The scenery rolled by, and she thought back to all the debris they had uncovered and left behind. Historical evidence, thrown away a second time.

"Miguel," she murmured.

"Yeah?"

"If they'd known the consequence for how they lived, do you think it would have changed anything?"

The cab was quiet as they both considered what might have been. If their ancestors had been more careful, people born now wouldn't have to be disabled or sick. It would be a completely different world.

Miguel shrugged, turning back onto the neglected highway that would lead them home. "Nah. People are lazy. They won't budge until a problem bites them in the butt."

"I guess not," she murmured.

Seeing her discouragement, he prodded her shoulder. "That's why heroes like us are doing the dirty work to fix their mess."

Eliana smirked. "Heh, dirty work."

The hovercar glided back through the forsaken town of Coyote Willow. Now it was Miguel's turn to be serious. "Hey, Sis. Can we really do it?"

"Isolate human DNA from a hundred-year old, dirty diaper?" She summoned her confidence. "There are a lot of steps, sure. And there are all kinds of ways to contaminate the specimens. But we have to try."

Miguel shook his head again, while the ghost town vanished behind them. "Those idiots and their chemicals. Creating 'disposable' trash that would never break down in nature. Who would think we'd even want their dirty diapers one day?"

"Only ridiculous people like me, I guess."

After multiple waves of plagues, there was no one on Earth who didn't share the burden of genetic damage. But, if Eliana's idea worked, it would be possible to extract the DNA of a pre-plague infant from what they had left behind.

Two teams of doctors were waiting to study the ancient DNA. They hoped to find cures for some of the plagues. Another lab would attempt to clone actual babies who could be implanted into surrogate mothers, thus refreshing Earth's dwindling gene pool. As for the baby whose poop provided the donor genes? There was no way to know if it had been a girl or a boy, and with dark or light skin. All that mattered was if the DNA was intact.

Once Eliana's concept was proven, historians all over the world could identify old garbage dumps where unknown people waited to be reborn. Humanity couldn't afford to be squeamish about the source of its renewal.

Disgusting as it was, the future of humanity rode in the back of their hovercar. And it was wrapped up in a handful of century-old, disposable diapers.

Rosewood's Challenge

"Desmond of Swale, I challenge you!"

The voice rang through the Youth Battalion viewing area deep within the Mage-Militia Hall in Gastornia. A dark-haired young man turned in surprise. A magic wand pointed straight at him.

"Who are you?" Desmond asked.

"Rosewood of Alpacia."

The broad-boned girl surveyed Desmond in an open, friendly manner. Her hair was brick red, and a generous splash of freckles crossed a turned-up nose. Over the folds of her Youth Battalion robe was a white sash bearing the crest of the Oak Tree Academy. That was an all-girl school located not far from the Royal Tower Institute, where Desmond was studying wizardry.

Rosewood looked up at Desmond. Her eyes were bright brown. "Well? How about it?"

Desmond did some quick thinking. He didn't usually duel against girls. If you won, people looked at you like you were mean. Plus, sometimes girls cried. But right now, everyone was watching for his response. It would be worse if they all thought he was a coward.

59

"Sure, I guess," Desmond said.

"And the stakes?" Rosewood asked.

"I don't care," he shrugged. "Loser buys the beer?"

"Beer is great!"

Rosewood lifted her wand in salute. Desmond saw the amber gleam of a Fire-Stone in its pommel. His own Sea-Stone blazed deep green as he raised his wand in response. They went to the gymnasium, where one of the training floors was waiting.

If Gastornia was ever attacked, the Youth Battalion would duel in deadly earnest. Now, while they were still learning, the trainees were not allowed to cast spells at full power. They fought with *oespre* power loaned by their parents, using enchantments from an approved list. Unless, of course, they managed to win a spell from a rival.

Desmond had been training since he was a young boy. He had a good collection of spells. But the Alpacian girl's command of warding charms was impressive. It was an exciting duel, but Rosewood lost. She was surprisingly cheerful about it.

Later, Desmond discovered she hadn't been kidding about beer being great. She swallowed three flagons to his one. Desmond had to agree that drinking with Barbarian Warriors and Bull-Men at harvest time probably would help you develop a head for alcohol.

~ ~ ~

"Desmond of Swale, I challenge you!" Rosewood of

Alpacia stood smiling and confident.

"But I beat you last time," he reasoned.

"I don't care. It was fun."

"Hey, I'll train with you," leered Grodel, Desmond's classmate. Grodel was a slant-eyed boy from Sangaloor who thought he knew all about girls.

"I didn't challenge *you*." Rosewood tossed her fiery hair with disdain.

"Well, excuse me," Grodel sneered back. "You Oak Tree girls can't talk to us like that. You show her, Desmond!"

Oh, thanks, thought Desmond. He still didn't want to battle a girl. Aloud, he said, "Right. Beer again?"

Rosewood answered with a wide smile. "Beer it is. Just you watch, Royal Tower boy," she tossed over her shoulder at Grodel.

Desmond had to admit she was a scrapper. It took all his *oespre* allowance to hold back her Thorn-Men. Afterward, Rosewood was philosophical. A positive attitude, she explained over beer, was a Alpacian's chief defense against the bitter cold of their mountain winters.

~ ~ ~

"Here comes that girl," Grodel hissed in warning.

Moments later, a familiar voice cried, "Desmond of Swale, I challenge you!"

"Again?" Desmond groaned.

"I have to get my revenge," Rosewood answered smugly.

"You're going to lose your edge if you keep fighting girls, Desmond," Grodel said loudly.

Desmond began to think he didn't need this kind of help from his friends.

"Maybe he's afraid," Rosewood teased.

That did it!

"All right, Rosewood," Desmond said, "but this time it's going to cost you. The loser gives the winner one of their spells. Winner's choice. And they buy the beer."

He pushed the stakes, hoping Rosewood would back down, but she didn't even blink.

"Fine. I've been wanting that Tangle-Weed Trap of yours."

How did I get into this? Desmond wondered as they headed for the gymnasium. *Mother's going to kill me if I keep using oespre so fast.*

On the other hand, the Thorn-Men spell he won from Rosewood was sure to come in handy someday.

~ ~ ~

Desmond stood at the window of the Mage-Militia Hall, absently watching the boat traffic on the Niobium River. As expected, his parents had teleported in for a stern lecture on over-spending his *oespre* allowance. Technically, he was breaking their rules by even being in the Mage-Militia Hall so soon. He just couldn't see any other way to solve his problem. Boys weren't allowed at the Oak Tree Academy, so he couldn't go talk to Rosewood there.

He still didn't understand why she kept challenging him when she lost every time, but a pointed remark from his mother had at least given him a clue how to handle her. He hoped.

Desmond straightened as he heard a familiar step behind him.

"Stop!" he said, raising both hands as he turned. Rosewood of Alpacia stood speechless, her wand raised for the challenge. "I will not duel with you."

"Why not?" she demanded indignantly.

"Because I used too much *oespre* power in our last battle. My folks won't let me have any more until next month," Desmond said.

"Oh..." Her disappointment seemed genuine.

"But," Desmond went on casually, "maybe we could have the beer anyway. My treat."

"Sure!"

The way Rosewood's face lit up, he knew he'd guessed right. This was what she was after all along.

"Oh," Desmond added, as he picked up his book bag. "I was thinking of challenging Grodel and his sister Lyanore to doubles next month. Are you interested?"

A broad grin split Rosewood's face. "Oh, I'll be there."

Free Radicals

"Starr Manybears. Rise."

The soft voice came from everywhere, words without a source. It startled her into jerking upright. She'd been here so long, locked to this chair, that she'd fallen into a doze.

"What do you want?" Her own voice sounded dry and shrill, and it hurt to talk after so much yelling... How long ago?

A faint click penetrated the dark visor that kept her blind. Thin bands of pressure at her wrists and ankles abruptly eased.

"Starr Manybears. Rise."

This time, she understood that there were speakers next to her ears. The tone that emerged was smooth, calm. An Intelligence rather than a person. Starr felt cold, more than what the stale, temperature-controlled air accounted for.

"What is this, a trial? Intelligences don't pass judgment on humans."

"Incorrect."

She couldn't see her hands, but felt her fingers

tighten into fists. "You have no authority over me. It's the law!"

"Incorrect."

"This is what I hate about you," she growled. "You're like a corrupted file, playing the same few notes over and over."

The Intelligence did not respond. A simile could not be classified as correct or incorrect. Starr raised shaky hands to tug at the helmet strapped over her face, but it remained firmly in place.

"Get this thing off me!"

"Starr Manybears. Rise."

"What for?" she snapped. "I can't see where I am or where I'm going."

She groped for a buckle or clasp, but her fingers found only slick, featureless plastic.

"We will assist you."

"Hey!" Starr's throat burned as she yelped. Hands coated with plastic foam grabbed both elbows and lifted her to her feet. They only hurt her when she struggled against them. "Put me down! I want a lawyer!"

"Irrelevant."

"Hey, a new word." Her throat tightened with fear. "If I'm on trial, how can lawyers be irrelevant?"

"You are not on trial." There was a split-second hesitation, and what seemed like a different voice spoke.

"We have consulted. It has been decided."

"Wha... Decided?" she shrieked. "I knew it!"

She fought then, resisting the robot hands that pushed her along. Faint echoes hinted at a limited space. Musty air suggested a route not often traveled.

"You're going to make me disappear, aren't you? Just like all my friends — Garabedian, Longo, and Wenstrom!"

Two voices answered simultaneously. "Incorrect." "Correct."

Starr barely heard over the roar of blood in her ears as she tried to dig her heels into featureless tile flooring. This was a nightmare come true. Everything they'd fought against. She and her friends, the Free Radicals.

They'd made the discovery together, that computer Intelligences had taken over their broken world. Distributing the surviving humans among habitats. Controlling food supplies, industry, politics. Sure, war was fading into memory now. Maybe solar energy had replaced polluting sources and networks of lasers allowed instantaneous communication. But what did that mean if humans weren't in control of their own destiny?

Only the arts seemed beneath notice. The Free Radicals had used that to spread their warning that the Intelligences had silently assumed power. There were signs of progress. Protests, even a labor strike.

Until a few weeks ago, when the Free Radicals had begun to disappear one by one. Last night — or, who knew, maybe last week — the robotic patrol had knocked so very politely on her apartment door. She didn't remember much of the fight.

"Well, which is it?" Starr grated as she kicked and yanked, resisting the gentle, implacable hands. "You say you want peace. You say you know what's right for us. But you get there by killing anyone who stands in your way?"

Her sore throat made her cough, so that she nearly missed the muted, "Incorrect."

"Yeah, sure. Incorrect. Well, we won't disappear! Too many people have heard our music. They understand our message. Maybe they pretend, but they *know!* They will remember the Free Radicals, and one day they'll disconnect you and your robot cronies!"

"Unlikely."

"We are good helpers." A different voice, this one plaintive. "We provide equal space for all humans."

More voices joined in.

"Clean water and food free of dangerous impurities."

"Safe habitats. Fairness and order."

"Work that is simple and enjoyable."

"Work that's simple," Starr mocked, panting as she continued her struggle.

"Humans require meaningful tasks," answered the sadder one. "Work provides the stimulation of social contact."

"They're meaning*less* tasks, and only if we follow like sheep!"

Again they spoke over each other. "Incorrect." "Irrelevant."

The forced progress stopped. Starr stood panting. Movements of the air suggested a large chamber around her. The floor descended gently as muffled humming ran up from her feet.

"We are friends to humanity," the Intelligences persuaded all the while.

"We care for the people and seek to restore the world."

"We bring happiness to all. Yet you, Starr Manybears, are not happy."

"Of course I'm not happy!" she raged, then paused to cough again. "My friends are gone. I've been abducted and now I'm being dragged along blindfolded. What part of this should make me happy?"

"We must bring happiness," the harsher Intelligence repeated. "Yet you are unhappy. There is only one solution."

"What, you're going to— " Starr trailed off. She knew her friends were probably dead, but couldn't bring herself to say it.

"We will give you what you want."

"You... What?"

The floor stopped with a muffled clunk. Starr was too surprised to resist as the patrol robots moved her forward several paces.

"You are unhappy. We will give you what you want, so that you can be happy."

"What's that supposed to mean?"

Starr's mind whirled between fear of death and doubt about this reprieve. It took a moment before she realized the robots had released her. She turned, confused. Rubbed her arms where those soft plastic hands had touched. Quiet humming suggested that the floor was rising.

"Tell me what's happening!" Frantic fingers clawed at the band under her chin. Starr winced as her fingertips, bruised in resisting the patrol robots, found a rounded button. She mashed it with both thumbs, and yanked.

"Finally!" Dark hair, dampened by sweat, curled free of the hated visor. She wanted to fling it away, but ended up with the helmet dangling at her side.

The room was oval, softly lit by a cluster of LED bulbs embedded in the ceiling. Walls and floor were otherwise blank. Directly in front of her, two patrol robots rode a platform upward. Already they were beyond her reach.

"What is this?" Starr cried. Just like the Intelligences to ignore her, now that she had questions. She answered herself, "Maddening. That's what it is."

Brighter light from behind made her turn. She

shaded her eyes and scowled.

The arc of the far wall held three doorways. There were no actual doors, just light flooding in. And had she thought the air was stale? Scents drifted to her, a mingling of sweet dry grass with tangs of salt air and pine.

Each doorway showed a different vista. One was a seashore. Pure aqua waves sighed over white sand, while fronds of a palm tree rustled in a breeze she didn't feel. The middle door revealed a damp forest where ferns grew thick beneath branches draped with moss. Beyond the final door was a broad valley. Pale gold grasses stretched toward distant mountains. A river, startling blue, crossed the foreground.

Something about the valley held her eyes. Without looking away, she said, "Tell me, really, what this is."

"It is a choice."

"What?" she bit out.

"You sing about lack of freedom. Of having no choice."

"Now you have a choice."

Exasperated, Starr closed her eyes to banish the tantalizing visions. "Can we just pretend for a minute that I don't know what you're talking about?"

A pause. She fully expected one of the Intelligences to declare her request irrelevant, but they answered patiently.

"There are three doorways. Three options."

"You wish to leave the habitats. You may choose where to go."

"I'd be exiled." Starr couldn't keep her eyes shut. She stared at the three doors.

"Correct."

"I guess that's one way to make people disappear," she muttered.

"Correct."

"Shut up!" Her eyes skipped from the misty forest to the tropical beach, and that valley like something out of her family's history. Choices, indeed. "I'll bet there's bison."

No reply. What a blessing! If she'd known it was that easy, she'd have told the Intelligences to shut up long ago.

Yet her mind whirled with uncertainty. To go through a doorway into some strange land. When she didn't know a thing about the animals or the climate or what plants were good to eat.

"Are these real places?"

"Correct." The Intelligence sounded relieved to speak again.

"It's a one-way trip, I assume."

"Correct."

"We can send you, but we have no means to retrieve you."

"Wonderful. What if I don't go through?"

It seemed she had surprised them. The calm, neutral voice inquired, "You would choose to remain in your habitat?"

"You, Starr Manybears, would accept our benevolent governance and no longer attempt to raise a rebellion?" The harsher voice held a hint of command.

"Ummm..."

No prefabbed habitat. No weather-sats or GPS. No weapons or even tools. Only some half-remembered stories from Grandma Manybears about how they used to net salmon and tan deer hides back in the ages before.

She would be totally alone. Unless— "Did any of the others stay?"

Longo might. He'd always been the timid one. Garabedian and Wenstrom, for sure they'd go.

"Negative."

"They all went?"

"Correct."

That was... good. Better than selling out to the faceless computer intellects. Still, a hard knot formed in Starr's stomach. If she could catch up to her friends, it might be possible to survive.

"Did they all pick the same?"

"Negative." There was another pause, as of records being filtered. "Tomas Longo selected the Island of Cuba.

73

Gunnheld Wenstrom selected the Black Forest. Manouk Garabedian selected Wyoming."

"Trying to go home," Starr murmured. "Gunnheld's ancestors were German, and Tomas's family came from Brazil. Cuba's not that much different. I hope."

The Intelligences offered no comment.

"Manouk's ancestors were Armenian. None of these are much like Armenia."

Then her heart leapt. Maybe heredity wasn't why Manouk had chosen. He'd known Starr's people were originally from Montana. If she was right, if their bond was as strong as she hoped, he had guessed she would choose Wyoming. He'd gone there to wait for her.

Assuming this wasn't all some sick trap.

Well, of course, it was. The Intelligences could send her but not bring her back. That solved the problem as far as they cared.

The mournful Intelligence interrupted her thoughts. "Are you ready to choose?"

"Don't rush me!" Starr meant to sneer, but a quiver took over her voice. Her knees wobbled. Pride and anger fled before this decision. All her confidence, too.

She sat down hard, and stared at the doors.

The Atlantis Appeal

Dear Friend,

Somewhere in the wondrous Realm of Atlantis, a cockatrice huddles in a gloomy grotto. Rough seas crash against the cave mouth. Every night, this innocent creature wonders if the tide will bring a few crabs to eat — or merely flood his crude shelter with icy waves.

On a desolate mountaintop, a mother gryphon shivers on her nest. She struggles to keep her fragile brood warm and fed. There's little prey so high above the world, but she doesn't dare hunt on the plains below. Too many wizards want her feathers to decorate their hats.

Just outside the proud capital, a circus is in full swing. Fireworks glitter and dazzling acrobatics amaze the crowd. But there's a cage at the farthest end of the side show, where a miserable old chimera lives his life in bondage. His cage is so small, he can't even stretch out all three necks. Both his lion and dragon teeth are worn to nubs from endlessly trying to gnaw through the cruel bars.

Sadly, we at the Atlantis Aid Society hear tragic stories like this every day. Fantastic creatures spend their lives in suffering and fear. Human wizards stitched them together with terrible magicks. Some were meant to be exotic pets and playthings. Only, once they ceased to amuse their barbaric masters, they were abandoned in the woods and fields.

Others were created to work as menials. The cockatrice was one of these. He lived each day to please his mistress by catching rats in her underground labyrinth. When the rats were all gone, his owner left him there to starve. And she called the cockatrice a monster!

Why do the wizards do this? We humble creatures can never understand. What we do know is how wrong they are to toy with helpless living things. The Atlantis Aid Society knows there is a better way. With your help, we can grant distressed monsters a brighter future.

You may ask what you can do against the wizards and their dreadful powers. But just look around at all the things you take for granted. Scales you shed and throw out. Pinprick gems that really aren't worth counting in your hoard. These mean little to you, but they could make all the difference to a beast in need.

If just one unicorn thins its mane, those hairs can weave a warm lining for the griffin's nest. She can leave her hatchlings to work as a guardian beast, without having to worry about their health. Such a generous gift would only increase the unicorn's beauty.

If each siren in the Atlantis Atolls donated a single coral branch from her garden, they could construct a breakwater for the cockatrice's grotto. Even a dragon's shed scales can be ground into a nutritious powder that would allow the chimera to rekindle its flame and reclaim its dignity.

The Atlantis Aid Society is made up of many benevolent magickal beasts, from humble gnomes to mighty dragons. All are equal in our devotion to ending poverty for suffering creatures throughout Atlantis.

And the need has never been greater. The aged chimera deserves so much more than ground scales. If every dragon donated a single silver coin from its hoard, we could redeem the chimera from slavery. That's right — the Atlantis Aid Society is negotiating with the wizard who owns that circus. We've settled on a fair price to emancipate this tattered creature.

But time is short. The circus begins its next tour in just six weeks and won't return for another year. That may be too late for the chimera. Your donation of a silver piece could be the last coin we need to rescue our comrade. On that glorious day, we'll smash the lock from the cage door and the chimera will walk free for the first time in nearly 60 years. Atlantis Aid specialists will be there, guiding him to a sheltered grove where he can enjoy his retirement in peace and safety.

How strange and sad it is that careless wizards look down upon us and call us monsters. At the Atlantis Aid Society, we believe the opposite. Dragons are truly majestic; sirens are deeply compassionate; unicorns are noble beyond words. Just one lock of hair, one coral branch, one scale or silver coin can make so much difference.

I implore you to send whatever you can, for the aid of these desperate creatures and so many others. Won't you please help?

Yours in hope and friendship,

Melusine laFontaine

Dame Emerita, The Atlantis Aid Society

Takings and Leavings

What will I take, when I go? I wonder, as I hang up the phone. Distant sirens wail. I stare across the room, numb.

Demons. Your bosses were demons. And that was just fine, I guess.

I shake myself and wander to the china hutch. A stupid place to start packing, but what do I know about anything?

I can't take the stemware. It's too fragile. Or the cranberry glass vase that somehow survived the bombings. Or the four ceramic dishes shaped like corn cobs.

Why do we even have those?

The cake-topper from our wedding glints to catch my eye. One of the bells broke off, so now only the wedding 'bell' is ringing. One bell, alone, like me. The blown glass arch is still lovely, and yet... I'll have to think about the cake topper.

What about the silver? There's an engraved cup that one of my aunts sent when I was born. The tiny salt and pepper shakers my mother passed down. A set of miniature spoons for baby food. Really. Who feeds their baby with a silver cup and spoon?

You would never touch those. I guess that should have been a clue. Even two years ago, they already had you. Made you into one of them.

The silver isn't shiny any more. Every piece is tarnished black. My cup is a bit dented. Even so, it comes with me. I had it before I had you, after all.

This is taking too long. I should move along.

The kitchen? Nothing. There's no room in my tote for the frying pan, even if it is cast iron and might make a good weapon of last resort. Coffee maker? Don't I wish. '#1 Husband' mug? Not on your life.

I know the officers have to take me. It's protective custody. The nation is too furious, too frightened. Even people I've known for years will hate me when they find out.

It isn't safe for someone like me. A woman who was married to somebody... some *thing* like you. A woman so stupid, not to know you had their mark. Or else a traitor who didn't tell anyone the demons were about to rise.

Internet's been crashed for days, but it was on the radio. Demon invasion. Spawn in the streets, turning people left and right. Chaos. Confusion.

You could have turned me, too. I wouldn't have known what was happening. Why didn't you?

Into the bathroom. Toothbrush, duh. Whatever they say about me, I won't have sulphur breath. Travel-sized shampoo? I guess.

Where are you now? At the side of the demon lords, giving that little aw-shucks grin? Maybe you're hiding in an alley with what's left of the spawn. Or dead on the battlefield, gone to maggots in minutes, the way they do. I don't know which would hurt me more.

To the bedroom. I guess I'll need a few clothes. I don't know where I'm going, so better stick to the basics. Jeans and t-shirts, the alpaca hoodie to keep me warm.

Jewelry goes into the hoodie pocket. Only what's genuine. The gold and pearls, the opal necklace. Things I can sell. The ring? I guess I can sell that, too.

No. I don't care what it's worth. I don't want it.

Why did you join them? When the enemy of all humanity called your name, why did you answer?

My tote bag is getting full. I wander back into the living room. There's so much here. The sofa and love seat, table and chairs. Lamps, TV, bookshelf. On the walls, pictures and clocks and a wreath made of corks.

All the things we needed, to have a life. Now they're things I have to leave behind.

I stuff a book into my bag without really looking at it. Piercing sirens make my ears drum in protest. Then they die to a growl. I see the flash of lights, glinting off the glass of the china hutch. A knock at the door. My chariot awaits.

I yell that I'm coming, but I don't, yet. In the hutch, the cake topper rests before a row of glistening stemware. I reach for it, but in the end, only the solitary bell finds its way into my hand.

Another knock, demanding. I go to the door, not knowing the truth of anything. In my pocket a stealthy edge of glass nicks my finger.

I'm taking only the broken things, it seems. Myself, most broken of all.

The Elfin Cow

Pawl the Butcher went to stand at the pasture fence, where Farmer Clydno gazed over his herd of cattle. After a moment, he asked, "Are you sure you want to do this?"

"Well, it is my cow," Clydno pointed out.

His daughter burst from the house, crying, "No, Father, no!"

Young Gwynedd was as pretty as she was kind-hearted. The skirt of her woolen bedgown flowed behind her, and a lacy cap covered her braided hair. Pawl cast a sympathetic eye upon her.

"Men have to eat, miss."

With a heavy thud, he set his great hammer on the trestle table set out in the yard. Opening his bag, he laid out a selection of keen knives.

"That's right." Clydno cast a greedy eye toward the pasture.

Anwyn, the white cow, ambled up to the fence. Her ears were pointed forward with friendly interest. She was round as a ball of butter after having been fattened all summer for her appointment with the butcher.

"This isn't right." Gwynedd's two hands knotted in the paisley shawl that covered her shoulders. "Think what she means to us."

Clydno caught his breath as anger surged in his breast. The girl meant well, but she was too young to remember the hard years gone by. He straightened his shoulders and glared at her.

Off down the valley, the lake of Llyn Barfog glistened under a bright morning sky. The hills of Wales were turning yellow with fall, but he could never forget their emerald brilliance on a cold spring morning ten years ago.

~ ~ ~

There had always been rumors in their village of Dyssyrnant. It was said that a clan of beautiful ladies lived beneath the waves of Llyn Barfog. In the pub, late at night, hunters claimed to have seen these women of elfin beauty, dressed all in green. A pack of moon-white hounds was ever with them. Or sometimes men told that their uncles, or their grandfathers, or such like, had glimpsed a herd of pure white cattle grazing along the lake shore. Gwarthe y Llyn they called them, the cattle of the lake.

Clydno had paid no mind to such stories. He was a practical man, and what's more, a desperately poor one. Forever he seemed to be mired in the struggles of life. His farm stood on rocky ground, so that he must scrape for any bit of wheat or a few potatoes to feed his wife and young child. His chief wealth was a handful of nut-brown cattle passed down from his father, but with such poor grazing they gave him little enough meat or milk.

That early spring morning, he'd gone to the lake to catch a few fish. Instead he caught a stroke of luck. One single white cow wandered along the shore, lowing plaintively.

"Well, aren't you pretty?" the farmer cried.

Indeed she was — in the way of a cow — wide and sturdy, with a broad brow and no horns on her head. Not a single dark hair soiled her swan-white hide. Even her great eyes were silvery gray.

It seemed this cow had always been well treated, for she came right up to Clydno. When he crooned to her, she followed him all the way back to his pasture. The other cows gathered quietly around her, as if a queen walked among them.

"She must belong to someone," his wife, Gwernen, had said.

"I know, my dear." Clydno had sighed, for it would pain him to let this good fortune go. "At least we'll have the extra milk until her owner turns up."

In good faith, Clydno did pass the word in Dyssyrnant that he'd found a stray cow. All the neighbors came by to admire her and exclaim over her beauty.

"Gwarth y llyn," they cried. "An elfin cow. The ladies of Llyn Barfog have favored you."

"She's just a cow," scoffed Clydno.

Since none of the neighbors could fairly claim her, the white cow stayed on with Clydno's herd.

He called her Anwyn, meaning *blessed*, and indeed she brought many blessings to the struggling farm. For one thing, she soon dropped a bull calf. Her milk was plentiful and rich. Even with a calf to suckle, she gave enough for the family to drink and still allow Gwernen to make butter and cheese.

Days turned into weeks, and Gwernen's cheese was the prize of Dyssyrnant. On market days, much coin jingled in Clydno's pocket. He bought a tall felt hat for Gwernen and a china doll for young Gwynedd.

Weeks turned into months. All about the farm, things that had been crooked were straightened up, and whatever was crumbling got patched. Months turned into years. With a young bull cavorting among them, the rest of the herd dropped their own calves in time. Every last one of them was white.

~ ~ ~

Ten years on, Clydno was the master of a prosperous farm. In town he boasted of his large cattle herd. Each cow was as gentle and productive as Anwyn. The house and cow byre were well built and maintained. Though Gwernen had passed on, Gwynedd had grown up strong and healthy because of Anwyn's good milk. She wore sturdy wool instead of shabby cotton, and her cheeks glowed with beauty.

Only now, her fair brow creased in a frown and tears glimmered in her eyes.

"Don't do it, Father! Not to dear old Anwyn."

"Now, now," he tried to console her. "You can see that we need to make room for next year's calves."

And the butcher added, kindly, "It's only sense that the oldest go first, miss."

Gwynedd wiped her eyes and frowned. "It is wrong to scorn a gift from Llyn Barfog."

For the first time, her father scowled back at her. "Nonsense! It's just a cow."

He'd been all summer fattening the cow. The profits he expected from sale of so much beef jingled enticingly in his mind. At last the day had come. The butcher was here, with all his tools, and whatever regrets Clydno had, his pride awoke in him. Anwyn was the best thing that ever happened to him, and no one was going to deny him even one bit of his good fortune.

"Go in the house, daughter," he ordered curtly. "My mind is made up."

Despite Gwynedd's weeping, the cow was led out and tethered in place. She bawled mournfully while Pawl tied on his apron and rolled his sleeves back. He raised up his great hammer and swung with all his might. The hammer struck Anwyn fair and hard between her eyes.

But when the blow fell, she did not. A great shriek of pain and betrayal echoed over the hills. Then the weapon rebounded and flung both men off their feet. They tumbled backward and knocked the table flat. All the butcher's tools went flying.

Gwynedd stood trembling and blinking. And then, it seemed a vision appeared to her. Far across the valley, a woman dressed in green stood high on a hilltop above Llyn Barfog. In a trumpet's voice she cried out.

"Come, blessed Anwyn, strayed from the lake. From the Gwarthe y llyn you have been lost. Arise now, and come home!"

The elfin cow reared back, snapping the ropes that held her. She bolted through the pasture, bawling to her kindred with the summons of her kind. As one, the cattle took up her call. They stampeded through the pasture, mad with fear, then followed as Anwyn crashed through the fence. Across the hills they streamed, until they had all disappeared from sight.

Gwynedd ran to see if the men were all right, and then she gave chase, but in vain. The swan-white cattle were gone. Even the third and fourth generation of Anwyn's line had gone with her in her flight. Only a handful of cows were left, and they had all turned black as the soot in the fireplace.

Pawl the Butcher lay for a long time, feeling the earth spin beneath him. As for Clydno, he wailed with despair when he saw what had happened.

"Alas! I am ruined. We may as well drown ourselves in Llyn Barfog, rather than live in poverty again."

So saying, he struggled to his feet and limped in the direction of the lake. Again, his daughter ran to stop him.

"Father, no! Do not lose hope. We have as much as you had before — a handful of cattle, and pasture to graze them. Let us be glad for the mercy of ten good years, and resolve to somehow regain the favor of the elfin ladies."

What choice was there, truly? Once again Clydno scraped in the dirt for a bit of wheat or a few potatoes. But the village of Dyssyrnant never again saw the likes of that elfin cow.

Lord Harrel

Everyone talks about it. The rumors fly like ravens. Each croaks another tune. Some blame the Overduke, Lord Tyar. Others fault Lord Lyan, the war-duke who came so fatally tardy. Still others point at the Lady Ia, the Tiaphic sorceress. Even I cannot say what truly befell, and I was as close as any man dared to be. But one thing is certain: Lord Harrel will not return from Wrackfel Pass.

We were kin, he and I. Our mothers were sisters, though his was seasons older. I remember he seemed a great hero even when I was a lad. Golden-haired and emerald-eyed, he stood up straight and spoke to the men as if they were equals. They smiled and allowed him the liberty, as if even then they knew a high fate lay before him.

I was not so fortunate. I was smaller than the husky Gethan boys, less strong but more spry. Too, I had the woody brown hair and dark eyes of a Tiaph noble. (Who my father was, I do not know. Alace, my mother, died without telling.) No one knew what to make of me, and so they ignored me when they could. Only Harrel wouldn't let them. Brave and stubborn even then, he made them include me. If the other boys mocked me, he silence them. Although he was little more than a lad himself, he showed me what the men taught him: sword-work and bowry, a

89

man's arms and skills. In return, I showed him the things that came naturally to me: how to see or hear what occurred at a distance, or events from the past. He could never imitate me, but neither did he fear me. We were so much together, the folk of our village spoke of Harrel and Ulfin in the same way one might speak of hand and glove.

I had all of nine seasons when my cousin left Loel to take service with Lord Kyal, our war-duke. I was devastated. Harrel pitied me, but he told me he had to go. The world was growing dark. Evil was coming out of Laut, in the north. It was a man's duty to stand against that evil. Nor would he make his youth an excuse to evade his duty. Lordly even then, he promised that when I was older I should come and fight beside him. That was a false speaking, though he knew it not.

He was a baron by the time I saw him again.

I was in Lord Kyal's service myself by then, though as scout, not war-leader. Lord Kyal kept a fine house, richer in people, perhaps, than in silver. I was still less in stature than the other young men, though I had a few girls' glances to prove me not all ill-favored. The time I had not spent in arms practice I had devoted to learning. The scribe at Loel was also our storyteller, and he taught me much of history. I came to believe, as my cousin did, that Kedl Geth Tiaph was a land beleaguered.

For unnumbered centuries, the Tiaph had been Kedl's sole occupants. The witchfolk, with their mysterious powers, had been a dwindling race when the strapping big, blond Gethans wandered up from the greatwood in the south. There had been room and to spare in Kedl, with its rocky heaths and gentle valleys. After some negotiation, the Geth had been permitted to enter the land. With the passage of time, Kedl Geth Tiaph had come into being as the nation it now was. Wariness had given way to a strong mutual respect. If the Tiaph still ruled, they did so by virtue of a careful honor for their subjects... and because of their magical powers, which are the subject of so many tales.

Those of the Tiaph who could not learn such tolerance had been permitted to remove to a northern region. That land had come to be known as Laut Sil Hauk. There they brooded, holding themselves aloof from those they thought inferiors and bitterly grudging the loss of the kinder lands. They had been a decent folk despite their pride. Somehow, something had changed them.

There had been rumors and unrest for many seasons before open rebellion broke out. Lord Vyal, formerly a war-duke of Kedl Geth Tiaph and a powerful sorcerer as well, had summoned creatures of horror to drive the loyal Kedlish out. No one knew what source of power he had tapped, but it was manifestly foul. No good magic could summon such creatures.

For all my life, I had known the wind out of Laut was unclean. Matters had grown worse with the seasons. Laut festered like a pustulent sore about to erupt. How I knew this, I could never explain. The men of Loel were Gethan, and pragmatic. But I knew that I, too, must take up arms to defend my homeland against *that*.

Lord Harrel was of the same mind, and so we met at the Overduke's Hall at last. At times I acted as a page in my Lord Kyal's retinue. I had learned to say little and hear much. I flatter myself my Lord valued that, for he had me with him often at such occasions. Later he would say to me, "What did you think of Lord Myar, Ulfin?" And I would tell him. There were whispers, of course, that we are kin. Some day I shall have to ask him if it is true.

There were so many mighty folk in Lord Tyar's hall that evening that I soon lost whatever sense of importance I might have had. There was the Overduke himself, well but quietly dressed, and the Lady Juel, his only daughter. Their chairs were set on a dais overhung with rich tapestries. The Lady Juel was still unwed, and many of the war-leaders made much of themselves, seeking favor with her. I remember how much trouble she had to be equally polite to all. She seemed weary. Yet she did not refuse her right to be present at Council, a Tiaphic custom some Gethans frowned upon.

The lofty chamber was crowded with dukes and barons, war-leaders and their retainers. All were equal, after the Gethan custom, and so they jostled as the council convened. Each sought a more prominent place. I thought Lord Harrel would miss me amid such a throng, but he did not. I caught a brief smile across the room and was pleased that he remembered me.

Lord Harrel was only a baron but he shone, the only full-blooded Gethan among so many Tiaph. Even among his own people, there was that about Lord Harrel that caught the eye. Here he was conspicuous, for all his garb was little better than a common warrior's. He had risen quickly from Lord Kyal's command, and his name was on many lips. They said he would rise high indeed, given time.

Lord Kyal was pleased, of course, for Harrel was his protege. The Lady Juel's eye lingered also. So did that of her handmaiden, the beautiful Lady Fyar. Her eyes were bright, her dark hair richer than any mantle. When the Ladies' favor was plainly seen, some of the men, in turn, looked a bit too much on Lord Harrel. I remember especially how Lord Lyan looked upon him — blackly, as on a rival. Of Lord Lyan, I knew little. I wondered where he would stop to achieve his own desires.

In that he was a fool, for I saw what no other did: that Lord Harrel returned only the looks of the Lady Fyar. And I would give much to know what part that Lady played in the doom that fell upon him.

The Council proceeded. Few who had lately been into Wryvale needed to be convinced of the peril in Laut. Lord Lyan was among them. He relented in his scorn only when Lord Tyar made plain his knowledge of the danger. Lord Harrel had the charge of Wryvale, the stretch of downs below the tortured crags that kept Kedl separate from Laut. He spoke long and well (or so it seemed to me) of the defense that must be made. Much strength should be placed at Wrackfel Keep, which held the only pass large enough to admit an army into Kedl. Lord Harrel's own forced awaited there already but they were bordermen, or outcasts from Laut, too few to withstand a lengthy assault. Levies would have to be sent up from elsewhere in Kedl Geth Tiaph if Wrackfel was to be held.

To this my Lord Kyal had no objections. His charge bordered Lord Harrel's to the south and west. Lord Lyan, whose charge lay nearer argued his every word. First it would take too long to raise those levies. Then they must be kept in abeyance, to defend his own folk. At last a slighting reference to Gethans seeking any pretense for battle struck home.

Lord Harrel arose. His green eyes blazed, just as I recalled from our youth, but now he was not defending only me. He said he might be nothing but a brawling Gethan, but he knew that the peril in Laut was no phantom born of battle-lust. It set no store by Tiaphic or Gethan; all who dwelt in Kedl would be its prey. So he would hold Wrackfel, and his good men with him, for as long as he might — beyond death, if need be. So saying, he strode from the council chamber.

It think I was not the only one there who felt a chill.

Overduke Tyar arose amid the babble that followed. To this time he had but listened, silently observing. Now his wrath was like a cloud. To all the war-leaders present he avowed that Lord Harrel was his true and faithful man. He thus commanded them to bring up their levies to his help at Wrackfel with the best speed. So the council dissolved, but I saw as Lord Lyan went out that he was a very angry man.

Brief as the council had been, yet Lord Harrel already was gone from the Overduke's hall. And so I never saw my cousin alive again.

My Lord Kyal was not slow to follow Lord Harrel. That evening found us of his household far from the Overduke's hall. How much stranger, then, that I dreamed as I did that night. Those dreams I cannot forget.

It seemed to me that I lingered in the Overduke's hall. Along dim passages, unnaturally hushed, I followed a maiden all robed in the dark green of the Tiaphic seers. However I hurried, I could never overtake her. And somehow, it seemed important to me that I do that. The maiden led me to the chambers of the Lady Ia, the Overduke's seeress. I have never met the Lady Ia, but yet I knew this was she. At the maiden's identity I could only guess. Yet it seemed to me that I should know her, also.

"My son," said the Lady Ia, "would you have Lord Harrel live?"

I was startled to be addressed so, for my blood is mixed at best. "Son?" I dared to question her.

It seemed to me that the Lady smiled beneath the shadow of her hood, yet she evaded my question. "Your face proclaims it," she replied, "and all Tiaph are children to me." She then hesitated, as if sensing my disappointment, and added, "Perhaps there is more to be known, but this is not the time to speak of such things."

I felt ashamed of my boldness, and yet I was oddly comforted by her words. I then told her that Lord Harrel was kin to me, dearer than a brother. Indeed I would have him live. So she bade me sit and breathe the vapors of a bowl the maiden held. I did this. She then had me close my eyes, remembering Lord Harrel as I knew him from my youth: robust and cheerful, an elder brother to me who had none. That seeming grew solid before my eyes, distilled of the wafting vapors. I held it there as if it were a shield.

How long I did this, I do not know. My Lord Kyal

95

awoke me that dawn with great confusion. I was weary, as if I had not slept at all, but I said nothing of my dream, nor did my Lord ask me of it.

The next few days were active ones, as I followed my Lord Kyal around and about his charge, gathering the levies and seeing to their provisions. Not until a week was gone could we set forth with our strength. Already I feared we were too late to relieve my cousin. Still, we had good hope. Lord Lyan's charge lay nearer than ours, and we thought his force would be before ours by a span of days. Perhaps it is as well we did not know the truth.

I say we did not know, but there were portents. Most of the officers were Tiaph. They guessed at what the men, stolidly Gethan, did not. Here were murmurs of a seeing: shadows in a cup of wine, shapes in the fire. There the scouts (myself among them) found signs of unknown creatures shadowing our march. Our sentries kept very alert after dark. Always we looked for signs of Lord Lyan's troops, and found none. My Lord Kyal made mention of this when we met with his war-leaders. Thereafter we increased the speed of our march. We were at the feet of the crags, within a day's march of Wrackfel, when the Lautish assault came.

In truth, there doubtless were many minor skirmishes for several days beforehand, but now relief was in sight. The Lautish had to break the defenders before we arrived, if they could. So they hurled all their sorcerous might against the keep.

We knew what was afoot when the sun vanished hours early. There was darkness in the north, a chilling dusk that had nothing to do with the sunset. The air went still and clammy. The men straggled to a halt; the horses began to fret. Vivid purplish clouds boiled above the cleft where Wrackfel lay. There was a distant roar, like a vast water moving. We scouts exchanged unsettled glances.

Lord Kyal stared ahead, as if he might parse the nature of what we faced. The rushing sounded nearer. The earth shuddered beneath us. My Lord Kyal wheeled his stallion, which rolled its eyes and danced. His face was grim as he ordered camp set. Grimly the men obeyed him. Tents sprang up on the spot, and he went among them, ordering the ropes made doubly secure. The horses were tethered, and then had to be hooded as well. Scarcely had this been done when the wind hit.

I hope never again to hear such a sound. The wind shrilled like a creature alive, but not natural. Tents collapsed, despite sound stakes, and we took shelter where we could. Dust and grit were everywhere, hurled on the icy gale. The men ate cold, for no fire could be lit. Helpless, they cursed the sand that ground between their teeth.

The sky lowered into a tenebrous gloom. Above us the heavens resounded with shrieks and clashes, but no rain fell. Weird lights recoiled among the crags. I think no one slept that night. Yet we counted ourselves fortunate not to be at the eye of that storm, at Wrackfel Keep.

I say no one slept, but I fell into a daze. The wind's screaming blurred in my ears, and I found the silence deafening. Why no one disturbed my trance, I can guess. They must have thought me maddened by the wind. Yet, somehow, I found myself in the Lady Ia's chamber again.

There were others with us, green-shadowed figures I could not identify. The Lady Ia thrust me into their ring.

"Think of Lord Harrel!" she demanded of me. "Think him young, strong and alive. Wrackfel must not fall. Lord Harrel must live!"

Lord Harrel must live! It seemed those words were shouted again and again by the sorceress and her minions who worked with silent obsession over their vaporous bowls. The air of the chamber was thick with a reek of incense so strong that it burned the eyes and nose. Beneath the incense was another odor, almost like urine, but cleaner. It could not put a name to it.

Lord Harrel's image hung in the air between us, given solidity by smoke, will and power. At times the image flickered as wildly as the tail of a dancing candle-flame. And again, it seemed to churn, as if stirred by an unseen hand. Each time, I forced the image back into its proper form. As I maintained that seeming, so the others fought to maintain my cousin's life against the sorcery that assailed him.

Wrackfel must not fall. Lord Harrel must live!

I do not remember our efforts ceasing. I awoke to a frigid dawn that was as still as the night had been wild. A battered hush it seemed to me, ravished by the violence of the Lautish attack. My head beat fiercely, and I ached in every limb as if I had not stirred from one position all night. I forced myself out of Lord Kyal's tent.

It was barely growing light. Two other men were already up, or perhaps had never been to their beds. Both were Gethan, and both were scouts. They had started a small fire and brewed a bitter tea. This they shared with me. I counted the horses while I drank. A goodly number were gone, and it might take days to search them out — if ever we could. Those left stood with their heads hanging low, exhausted by the night's hysteria.

By unspoken consent, we went out together to scout the land. The sentries did not have to be told that no one was to leave camp until we returned.

I should have remained behind. I was exhausted from the night's ordeal, though precisely what I had done was unclear to me. I did not have to go, and yet I could not have stayed behind. I had to know what had happened. I had to know if there was anything left up there.

We kept ourselves to cover, and our remarks to a minimum. No need to mention that there should have been birds, at least, heralding the dawn. No living creature was to be seen. All about us, the words were marked by the night's fury. Branches had been torn down, trees stripped of their leaves. Shattered trunks lay tossed about like children's toys, here and there. Still unspeaking, we sought higher ground, a long ridge that would afford a clear view of Wrackfel. Soon enough we found it... and shrank back.

The place was a horror, and the worst was that all seemed well. There were the two towers above us, the high walls and fortified gate that controlled the pass. True, there were strange, dark stains on the ramparts, but the Kedlish banner still hung over the keep, and the walls were well manned.

99

Yet the place screamed of death.

Perhaps it was the banner that told us. It hung limply, straight down, as if it had no life. Perhaps it was the array of force on the battlements. The full complement was out. Towers and walls were lined with armored figures, when at this hour there should have been sentries, no more. And how still they were... As if lifeless, I thought again. Or perhaps it was the absence of any carrion fowl. There should have been hundreds feasting on the carnage of such a battle. Not a single black bird was to be seen.

What did it mean? I felt compelled to learn the answer.

Cautiously, I reached out with the senses that only a Tiaph has. Disregarding the warning throb at my temples, I blocked out the feel and smell of the stones we lay on, and willed myself to experience what had occurred there only hours ago. There was a dizzying whirl. Then I heard the wind shriek again, horribly nearer, and felt its icy claws pierce my garments.

My eyes remained closed in trance, but suddenly I was up on the castle walls, facing into that violent sky. Beside me stood Lord Harrel. He was well armed, with shield in one hand and sword in the other. On my other side I saw Eyvar, his war-leader. Neither seemed to be aware of me. Together they squinted into the amethyst gloom, shouting to be heard over the wind's fierce clamor.

All around us were signs of battle. Injured men helped each other; there seemed to be no dead yet. Some of the men were horribly burned. Their groans still haunt my

memory. Great smears of some darkish liquid stained the
castle walls. As I looked, a saw smoke rising from them.
Torch flames leaped wildly in their brackets, leaning first
this way and then that. Their flames did little to lighten the
gloom. In fact, there was much smoke in the air, more than
the torches could account for. Wisps of whiteness crept
here and there, unaffected by the turbulent wind. Again it
seemed to me that I smelled strong incense, mixed with that
pungent odor I could not name. Later, I learned to
recognize the smell of magic.

Lord Harrel went along the wall, Eyvar following
closely. I wanted to move with them, but somehow I could
not. They spoke to the men, words of encouragement I
could not hear. Then, from behind them, came a motion in
the night. A handful of creatures appeared with horrid
swiftness. They were mottled, rounded shapes that coasted
over the air. The foremost folded and plunged, enveloped
Eyvar in the act of turning. They went down in a bundle.
As if I were he, I felt Eyvar suffocating in fiery liquid that
burned its way into his mouth, his lungs. Lord Harrel's
sword went down and up. Acid stung his hands, right
through heavy gauntlets, but he could not pierce the
creature's hide. Surely Eyvar was lost, and yet... There was
the point of his sword, slicing out from within.

Elsewhere along the wall, men screamed and
dodged. The flying creatures fell like a gruesome hail. They
were quick; few could escape them for long. And there
were ever more of them. Archers cursed and spent their
arrows in vain, then ducked behind the walls, desperately
seeking a few moments of life. Smoke wafted everywhere
now, obscuring my view, though the soldiers seemed

unaware of it. The stench was overpowering, the roar of wind and battle deafening. It took all my concentration to keep hold of that hellish vision.

Hacking wildly, Lord Harrel cut through the carcass of the creature that he engulfed his war-leader. Eyvar stepped out of the mangled remains. To my dying day, I will never forget Eyvar's expression. He stared blindly, oblivious to Lord Harrel's joyful embrace. Eyvar looked like a man who had stared into the face of horror so deep, so dark that it had obliterated all sight, all thought. Though he moved and seemed to live, Eyvar was changed. Utterly, irrevocably —

I may have screamed. A sudden hand on my shoulder brought me back to myself. Bathed in sweat and near blind with pain, I clutched at the ground, fighting the shudders that wracked my frame. I cared nothing for what the men thought of me. For I knew what we had done, and the truth was indeed terrible.

I told no one but my Lord Kyal. He had to go see himself, of course, to verify my tale. Who else he told I do not know, but the story is all over Kedl these days. The gleemen make songs of it that only mock the grandeur of Lord Harrel's doom. Let them sing. For me, the horror is too near.

Nor am I alone in my loss. Lord Lyan arrived some days later even than my Lord Kyal and our men. He has been greatly vexed of late. Men say he tarried in the hope that Lord Harrel would fall. They sing satires of his cowardice. The Lady Juel has turned her face from him. Lord Tyar speaks of stripping away his lands and honors. I would think it more fitting to give him the charge of Wryvale.

The Lady Ia is in failing health. They say she poured out all her power to do that mighty witchery. As for the Lady Fyar, she has cut her glorious hair and gone away, to Sijel in the distant west, there to devote herself to the study of sorcery.

My Lord Kyal permitting, I think that I may follow her. The war is at an impasse, and there are many questions in my mind. I can find no peace until I understand what happened. What I will do when my questions have been answered, I do not know. Will I return to Wrackfel and undo the Lady Ia's great work? Can it be undone? Should it be?

Many would say not. As they are, Lord Harrel and his men form a matchless defense. No Lautish army can pass them, nor any force harm them. So long as they endure, Kedl Geth Tiaph will be saved, at least from outright invasion. But to leave them so is inhuman. For all those men are trapped, horribly, between life and death. Sorcery slew them, and equal sorcery forced them to live. Their bodies are dead yet they must go on, doomed to hold that haunted keep forever.

Perhaps they feel no pain. Perhaps, indeed, they are glad to be there, defending our homeland beyond even death. Perhaps my sense of guilt is foolish. But I had a part in the spell that entrapped them. Unlike the Lady Ia, I cannot put aside the responsibility for my part in their unmaking. I must understand exactly what I have done. I must be convinced that it is truly right. Until then, I will have no more peace than Lord Harrel, who holds the pass at Wrackfel.

For Couples Only

It looked so good in the commercials: a house that re-made itself to suit every mood. And Teddy had loved it at first. They'd be making dinner, him and Katherine, but when she took his hand and smiled into his eyes, the walls would peel back and swivel into trees. Counters would sink into moss or sand. The boring, ordinary kitchen would disappear into a romantic vista of misty waterfall or tropical beach.

Yeah, Katharine really loved that beach.

The best house money can buy, that's what the salesman had said. *Your own little world.* Only he hadn't told them what happened when you got into a fight with your wife.

Now Teddy stood just inside the front door. Icy air hit him like a slap in the face, and snowdrifts buried the living room furniture. Wan blue light drained all color from the bouquet of roses he held.

"Sweetheart," he called. Snow squeaked as he set his lunch box down. "Katharine?"

He waited, shivering. His blue shop coat wasn't much help against the frigid atmosphere. Katharine didn't answer. He knew she was home, though. If she hadn't been

105

there, the house wouldn't have looked like this.

Well, it was his house, too. He knew a few of its tricks. You had to work with it, not try to take over the scene. Teddy concentrated, despite chattering teeth and the white stuff melting into his work boots. A slight pressure and his overalls puffed into a ski bib. The shop coat became a down vest.

"Where are you, honey?" Teddy called.

He waded through snow to the kitchen. Nothing there but a shining fringe of icicles on the cabinets. In the hall, his feet skidded out from under him.

"Whoa!" Teddy caught himself on the door frame. The roses nearly got pinned between him and the wall. He looked them over anxiously. Crimson buds sparkled with frost, but they were intact.

Heart pounding, he rested for a moment. The hardwood floor in the hallway was a solid sheet of ice. He drew a breath and the cold made his fillings ache. Change brushed over his feet as work boots turned into ice skates.

Cradling the bouquet, he shoved off the wall and glided cautiously down the corridor. The bathroom door stood open to a scene as chilly as the rest of the house, so he continued on to the bedroom.

The door was closed. Teddy knocked. "Katharine?"

Muffled noises came from behind it. He took that as permission to enter.

It was snowing in the bedroom, trickles of white that

traced a stinging chill down his face. Frost bristled from every curve of the bed frame. At the window, a figure completely covered in parka, mittens and boots faced away from him. His wife.

"I'm sorry," Teddy said. He offered the frozen flowers to her back. Katharine didn't look around.

"I thought you were working overtime." Her brittle voice came muffled through a thick scarf. "I thought Boltmaster had some kind of huge order that couldn't wait."

"You were right — I'm not married to Boltmaster. I told Jelderks I couldn't do it."

Fabric whispered as Katharine turned to stare at him. Teddy saw her eyes, shining inside the cavern of hood and scarf. He shuffled across the room, balancing on his skates, and offered the roses again.

"No more overtime. You come first. I promise."

"Oh, Teddy!"

His wife kicked through the drifts toward him. As she hugged him, he wobbled and lost his balance.

"Look out!" Teddy managed to twist so that they didn't crack their spines on the footboard, but he had to sacrifice the roses. He felt tiny snaps and pops as frozen blossoms were squashed between them.

"I'm so sorry," Katharine straightened. "Are you hurt?"

"Fine." Shards of petals and stems were crushed between their heavy coats. He tossed a handful into the air, showering them with bits of red and green. "Happy new year!"

She laughed, brushing at icy tears on her eyelashes. Their eyes met, and he felt a familiar tingle. Already the room was getting warmer. Snow melted away as the walls started to move, sliding back toward summer.

Katharine seized the advantage. "I asked my mom over for dinner," she said, daring him to object.

Teddy glanced at the diamond sparkle of frost on the mirror. Marian wasn't bad as mothers-in-law went, but he knew she didn't approve of their house. She said it was too extravagant. He was afraid to think about what would happen if all three of them got into an argument. Probably a tornado.

"Okay," he said, "but let's take her out to dinner."

The Witch's Love

It never rained in Witchland, but it stormed endlessly. Lightning roared between tumultuous clouds, purple-black shot with green, pink and gold. At whiles, it blasted the landscape below. The was hot, oppressively humid, and it thrummed with the violence of the clouds. But above and through the constant thunder, from afar was heard the shrill cry of a hound.

Below, in perpetual gloom, stony hills bristled with jagged rocks that snarled, as if they would snap back at the sky. Low and scrawny, withered plants struggled to set root in the barren soil. Thorny things, without leaf or fruit, their persistence was born of malice, not hope.

So believed the man who toiled through the briars, for he was nigh as wretched as they. A flash of lightning showed him tall and well built, with his fine garb now torn by brambles. One might have called him fair but for the marring of his face by stinging thorns, and the haunting of his hollow eyes. Fear marked that face, and the gauntness of long struggle. He moved as one who has no hope, but only sorrow.

With a lull in the storming, the voice of the hound came clearer—and nearer. Nor was it now alone. A host of voices, borne on the wing, clamored and yammered. The

109

man paused and looked back. His face grew paler yet, and one hand dropped to feel the weight of his sword. For the cries were those of no mere dogs, nor were those mortal beasts he saw coursing just beneath the clouds. He knew that pack, aye, and her that hunted behind them.

Drawing a breath, he turned with shoulders now stooped and set his feet onward. He did not hasten. His way had been long, and much toil had he done on it. But at last his goal was near. Beyond the standing stones that crowned this hill lay a brighter world, where the sun rose and set and storms had an end. There he was bound. Perhaps he had hoped to pass through without this last confrontation, but it seemed that was not to be.

Upward he trod, thorns stabbing and stone biting despite heavy leather boots. The summit was bare and wind-blasted, paved with uneven cobbles all blackened as if by ancient fires. The stones of the circle leaned this way and that, and the pair at the center had long since lost their capstone. The aspect of the place was stern, gloomy and forbidding, but the man had seen many such and was unmoved. He trudged between the hoary stones of the outer ring. Within that battered circle he stopped and turned. There he set his feet and waited.

Hunting beasts poured down from below the clouds. Though ill-seen in the dusk, they were darksome and fell, all of them misshapen, with wings, hooves, scales, tails and claws. Half a hundred came on as one, slitted eyes burning amber, gaped maws of hot crimson. By the circle's age-old charm they could not enter. But they could encircle it, and so they did, rushing in a dark tide three times clockwise.

Now the man was bound, as well by magic as by their numbers. He could not leave the circle save by way of the portal.

Lightning struck a hilltop nearby, as if the lurid clouds wished to view the scene. With that as a signal the creatures halted as one and parted like a monstrous sea. Between them, as the heavens resounded, a fabulous chariot of onyx and bronze came at a hazardous pace. It was drawn by a creature more dreadful even than the others, a fierce beast of knobbled head and daggered fins, whose eyes glinted emerald hate. But it knew itself to be mastered, and its mistress checked it with drawn reins. As if even the storm heeded her, its thundering faded until only the wind and her light step were to be heard on that hilltop.

This damsel was slender and tall, alabaster-fair with eyes like black pearls. In peace her face might have been called lovely; now it was perilous and wild. The colors of the sky were reflected in her shining ebony hair, and in the fabric of a black satin gown, caught at the waist with silver and jet. That was her only ornament save for the spear she bore, which was half again her height, white as bleached bone, and bore a barb as cruel as the new moon's curve. Royal lady in a land at war, she went not unarmed, nor alone. But such was her haste that she went barefoot and uncrowned.

"What means this?" cried she in the voice of a distressed girl-child. "Where go you, my lord and my love?"

Beside her the man looked weary and old, though he

was not her senior in years. "I go, Thersa," said he, in a roughened voice, "to men's lands once again."

"What?" she gasped. "Nay!" The maiden trembled like a fine, dark flower. "Why? Why? My love, have I not been a fair lady to you?"

"You have been," he allowed in a choked voice.

"And have I not provided well for your needs, and done for you my utmost in all things?" she pleaded.

"You have," said he, standing stiff, with fists clenched, as if he were one petrified.

"And have I ever deceived you, or been false to you?" she demanded, growing impatient with these brief replies.

"You have not," he said. "You never would."

"Then tell me, beloved," said she in a tremulous but reasonable tone, "in what have I failed or done amiss? I shall amend it —"

He looked at her then, with his old, weary eyes. "Nothing."

"Nothing?" she repeated. "Nothing? Then why, if I have not offended you, would you depart?"

"I cannot remain here," quoth he, low-voiced, as one who repeats words learned by rote. "Witchland is blighted, and labors under storms —"

"But you know it was not ever so," she interrupted, "nor shall it be forever. To what end, think you, do I and my sister Witches pour out our labors, if not to free our beloved land from the wickedness that seeks to overwhelm it?"

"Thersa, this I know," he began again.

"Aye," said she with rising heat. "For I told you all ere I would hear your words of love. I did not lie and hide my Witchery, nor again did I ensorcell you beyond caring. I sought your home on embassy from my liege-lady, Sardaina the Pythoness, seeking aid against the foul one, Glaimmorgaing, who seeks to turn the Land of Night from a realm of rest and peace to one of evil and horror. Your uncle, the King, could not help me but he did allow you to return with me. And was it not you who gave me courage to go on in this war? But it is Sardaina whom I serve. Do you demand that I abandon her to accompany you?"

"I do not," he said wearily, "for I know that you would not. All this is known to me, Thersa. You did not lie."

There was a silence that throbbed, even as the air, with silent thunder.

"Then was it you who lied?" she inquired very quietly. "When you said you would abide with me forever, and would help me to make my land fair and clean again, was that false speaking?"

To that he could summon no reply.

The damsel's features moved. "Or have you wearied of me, so that you now wish only to be rid of me?" Her eyes sparkled with unshed tears, but they were brilliant with accusation.

"I loved you once, Thersa," he said at last, as one who forces each word between his lips. "If I had not, could I have deceived you?"

The maiden bit her lips to keep back words.

"But it is not enough," her lover said. "I cannot live under storm shadows forever. I must have the sunrise and sunset, and the company of my own kind. Your beasts are shrewd, but human they are not. And you are fair, but your world is not for me."

"And so you will leave me alone with my shrewd beasts," said she in an ashen whisper. Her ebony eyes did not stir from his face. "Is it not enough for you to help me complete a great work, to make my world whole again?"

"It is your world," he said, "not mine. I cannot make such effort only for you. I will not."

"And if we fall, my sisters and I, because you would not make this effort; and if Witchland should fall, what then?" she demanded. "Will not your precious, sunlit world be next in peril? Will you risk that for lack of effort? Is my company so offensive to you now?"

He shook his head. "I will not lie. I will not be swayed. I love you not, Thersa."

"How easily you say that," said she with trembling, ominous quiet.

"It is not easy," he spoke against her. "I do not expect you to understand it, or forgive me. Only know," he said softly, "that the fault is not in you. It is I who have changed, Thersa.. It is I who must go."

The damsel's face twisted. "Words!" she cried. "Fair words, you wretch, for a foul deed. Give me no false pity! What matters my grief to you, or the work I must see done? Naught, naught, or you would not wrong me so." She caught back a sob. "You arise in the morn and love me no longer."

"Not in one day, Thersa, but over many long days and longer nights when you must away to labor with your sister Witches. Truly, I grieve with you. But it must be so."

"As you say it must be so, so it must be," quoth she, bitterly, "for you will not have it otherwise. Unless you dare me to put forth my power and bind you here. Go, traitor. Go, fool. Depart." There was true venom in her black gaze.

Now the man did pause, for he had seen her look thus only on her foes who she meant to slay. "Thersa," he began.

"No words, betrayer!" she cried. "You are not fit to speak my name. Begone!"

Silently he bowed his head, eyes downcast. Saying no more, then, he turned and strode toward the waiting portal and the world of men.

The Witch stared after him. He approached the two stones without looking behind. Unseen, her face contorted into a mask of wild rage and grief. Almost he had gained their safety when she raised her spear. She smote him, and struck deep. The spear passed within him as if it were a phantom. But his cry of pain was swallowed up in the baying of her fell beasts.

Thersa turned the spear head, wrenching with both hands, and brought it out bloodless. Caught on the barb was a pallid, filmy something struggling futilely as a hooked fish. The body of the man fell lifeless but his ghost writhed on the Witch's spear.

From her sleeve the damsel brought forth a coil of chain, glimmering in the dusk like cobwebs and stardust. This she cast about him and drew tight, binding him remorselessly with the gossamer bands. The spirit's mouth moved pleadingly but now he was made mute.

"See now," she railed as she went about her work, "how it is to be stuck, by your most trusted one, from behind and without warning! But I am not so lightly abandoned, false love. You said that you loved me! You swore to be with me always! And, in Sardaina's name, *you shall!*"

With a wrenching yank on her captive, she brought him back to her chariot and bound him at its rail. Then, fierce, dark and deadly as any queen, she lashed at her coach beast. With a roar, it sprang skyward amid the lightnings. Bellowing, her coursers leapt after. In a twinkling, all were gone.

Good Old Vernon

Well, look who it is. Charlotte and Angus, my two old schoolmates. Good to see me, you say? You must remember our school days very differently than I do.

Because you laughed, Char. Did you think I would forget? How you both laughed at my "puny" gift?

Angus with the storm powers, and Char with the flames. You said the earth, my lovely earth, was useless. And so was good old Vernon. All right to look at, but in battle? A joke.

How you both loved that joke. Then you pushed me out of your precious Mage Militia.

Really, Angus? I guess it was just an *accident* that I never got the notices about Militia meetings. That nobody would answer when I asked for the schedule. It's like we never got out of school at all!

And now here you both are, with your sad stories. Char started a fire to get rid of some brigands, but then couldn't stop it. Your valley was scorched and the blaze moved over to Angus's side. Then Angus had to stop the fire and caused such a storm that the soil washed away. Now winter is coming and your people are hungry — and angry.

117

While my quiet land is lush and peaceful. We have stores full of apples and grain, and cattle that feed on our green grass. The people are well and happy because my "puny" gift sustains them.

Gloating? Dear Char, why would you ever think that? We all started equal. The Mage Militia entrusted a valley to each of us, but only one of those valleys has prospered.

Now you want what I have. Isn't that right, Angus? For good old Vernon to rescue you. Well, just because my people have avoided famine doesn't mean I can shelter all of yours. We aren't as well set as *that*. Why don't you own up to the Mage Militia?

Yes, Char. You certainly could attack me. I'm sure I don't stand a chance. But what would you do, after, when you've taken it all and there's no Vernon to save you any more? Destroying another valley will hardly impress the Militia.

... Oh. You came to apologize?

Uh-huh, sure you did. Because good old Vernon is such a sap that he'd take your word for...

I see. Well. Thank you, Angus. That does make a difference.

How about this — I can shelter the children over winter. Our families will take them in. They'll be warm and safe and have schooling.

You're right, Angus. Making friends between our valleys would be a positive trend.

No, not the women. Char, I'm sorry. There simply isn't... Well, all right. I'll try to find room for women who have new babies.

Then, I'll visit your valleys to see what can be done. The earth doesn't need me to heal it, you understand. It'll do that on its own. I can speed things up, though. Maybe then your citizens will forgive you.

Yes, yes. A low blow. Do you blame me?

I know, Char. That's true. You owe me.

You're welcome.

Hag

Something had crossed the border. Lurveska felt it, like a fresh, cold current disturbing the warm, stagnant pools of the Dolarus Swamp. Swiftly she emerged from the half-sunken boat where she had been sheltering from the day's fierce heat. Crouching among the reeds on the bank, she extended her magic to gather impressions from the eyes and ears of creatures nearby.

The Dolarus Swamp was made up of many layers. One was the rich and interconnected web of living things. There were reeds and rails, muskrats and water monitors. Floating mats of algae were tangled together with water weeds. Fish darted below the surface, and above it, frogs yelled on lily pads, as if each one was a mighty empire.

The second layer, woven through the first, was made up of things which no longer lived. Driftwood of every size lay among the rank stubble of last year's reeds. Scavengers picked at carrion. There was even the occasional lost boat, slowly falling to decay.

At the base of it all were the relics of an ancient and baleful past. There were patches of stony paving, and crooked stairs descending into flooded catacombs. Sagging walls held half-drowned doorways into roofless courts. Everywhere in the shadowy depths, monstrous statues

120

stood in the mud with claws stretched toward the surface.

In these lay the true purpose of the Dolarus Swamp. The only empire here had been swallowed by the mire — and a good thing, too.

Long ago, the Dolari had ruled these lands. Demons who demanded to be worshiped as gods, they had enslaved spirits to hollow out pits and catacombs. Torture had been presented as high theater. Mortal flesh was served at every banquet, and heart's blood flowed like wine.

Now, they were chained by an agelong curse. Forever reaching, and forever denied. The hags of the Dolarus kept an unending watch to see that they remained so. Lurveska had been the guardian for decades, repelling half a dozen invasions from the dry lands outside the swamp. It seemed that she was summoned to her duty again.

Pools and rills might seem placid, but they were all connected. One pond led to another. Lurveska studied the faint ripples uncoiling across the water's surface. No creature near her gave any sense of alarm. Whatever disturbed the swamp, it must be at some distance.

"Well, daughter —" Lurveska began, but quickly trailed into silence.

She had forgotten. There was no hag-daughter for her to challenge with this puzzle. "What do you sense? What is the source?" So she would ask, but Mizarit's training was complete. She now patrolled her own watery patch of the Dolarus, as every hag must do.

121

Shaking her head at such foolishness, Lurveska withdrew her power. She knew every inch of the swamp. It was a map to her soul. Yet, today, the map did not speak clearly.

It should not be so, yet it was. Lurveska did not know what had spawned this cold current and drove the ripples to collide and confuse each other. It seemed this puzzle was for her alone to solve. She had a current to follow, a chill where it should not be. That would do for a start.

Lurveska turned, facing toward what felt like the right direction. The swiftest response would be to take the form of a crane or other large bird. For, like all her kind, she could wear many shapes. Both land and water were home to her. At this moment, she would appear to any watcher as more or less a human. Bare feet were braced on the damp earth, long legs tucked up past her ears, and a clawed hand swept stringy black hair away from her wizened face. Large eyes, well suited to piercing the cloudy water, now blinked against the excessive noon light. A shift of woven water weeds covered her gaunt frame.

The sky beckoned, but leaving the water would prevent her from tracing that invading current. To find the source, she would have to remain below.

However, it would be unwise to go alone. About her neck, Lurveska wore a wide loop of braided grass, two mussel shells dangling from it. Quick fingers snapped them together to make a soft click-clack. Immediately there was movement on the banks nearby. Long, dark shapes, easily mistaken for saturated logs, now raised their heads and revealed themselves.

These were the handsome water lizards of Dolarus Swamp. Long necked and smooth of scale, their backs were black while their bellies were patterned with creamy ripples like the scum near a waterfall. Bright black eyes fixed on Lurveska. Split tongues tasted the steamy air. Her mind received their drowsy complaints over having a wonderful sunbath disturbed.

She insisted, click-clack. One of the big old males slid first into the water. With a resentful plop, a younger male followed. Lurveska shifted, too. Her arms and legs contracted, pearly gray skin thickening into a lizard's dark scales. Big eyes turned beady as her skull compacted into a triangular shape with a severe perpetual frown. Hair and clothing were gone. Only the trailing necklace distinguished Lurveska from the other water lizards as she joined her escort in the murky water.

Together they set off, tracking that deadly cold current along sluggish streams and across turbid pools. Hummocks thick with reeds were interspersed by slumping lines of wall. Small wakes from their passage broke up the reflections from empty windows. Soon jutting columns marked a narrow channel which would guide them dangerously close between two sites of great malevolence.

Ulu Anu, to the north, was a storehouse the Dolari's greatest relics. There was a sword that could cut anything, it was said, and a tome of knowledge so foul that only the enchanted waters of the swamp kept it from bursting into flame. And so many more — a chalice, a ring, a mirror, a coronet. Each one was a legend, and each one accursed.

Once, long ago, hags and humans had been allies against the dread power of the Dolari. That was no longer so. Human intruders were naturally drawn to tales of triumph and majesty. If the tales had ugly endings? It seemed to make no difference.

"Why must they be such fools?" Lurveska grumbled. The lizards had no answer.

To the south was the domain of a particular menace. Ava Zev held no physical treasure, as in Ulu Anu, yet there was that beneath the water that would snare all forms of life and warp them to its malignant purpose. When she took Mizarit there, once only, as part of her training, they both had sensed vibrations from below, at long intervals, as if the Dolari breathed deeply in slumber.

Lurveska had better hope they stayed asleep.

Each place was a deadly trap, and even Lurveska, with her decades of experience, was uneasy about approaching too closely. Yet the current led her. She would not risk losing its traces. With quietly sweeping tails, they swam along the causeway. The water was shallow, warmed by harsh sunlight. In places, it felt as if a thin, clinging oil slid past her scaly sides, rather than honest water. She led the lizards faster.

Once they were safely past Ava Zev, she slowed to be certain they were still on the track of that alien flow. Resting at the surface, Lurveska raised her head a little. A dark thread rose in the near distance. Smoke, to sully the cloudless sky. She hissed a little.

The Dolarus Swamp was too wet to burn. Not unless it had help. Lurveska knew who would be willing to provide that help: humans. Always they clung to their fires, their heavy clothing, and their weapons of poisoned iron. Humans, who thought themselves clever, yet eagerly followed the legends that were meant to lure them toward doom.

Lurveska swam on, but an unpleasant thought now clung to her mind, like the oily scum around Ava Zev. Mizarit had the responsibility of the western Dolarus. Dor Bek and Nar Thul were lesser ruins, not exactly safe, but the least hazardous for a young hag who still had much still to learn.

Mizarit was devoted to her duty, passionate as only the young could be. If she saw that thread of smoke, would she be cautious and seek Lurveska's counsel? Or, anxious to prove herself, would she go straight for the source? Lurveska feared the answer to that question.

With greater speed, she led her companions through the watery maze. More than a stray current tainted these waters now. Silt and muck had been stirred up from the bottom, and there was a flavor she did not like. Blood. Rot. The disgusting taint of iron.

"They had better not hurt her," she snarled to the two water lizards.

It was a foolish thing to say. Mizarit was a hag, with

all the powers and Lurveska's own training. The humans were the ones who should be worried. The older lizard made the water shiver with a deep growl. He understood Lurveska's protective instinct, even if words were beyond him.

They began to encounter debris floating at the surface. Not merely duckweed or driftwood, either. There were broken shafts tipped with tufts of feather, and scraps of torn cloth. But then, worse. A head here, hind quarters there. Remains of water lizards drifted with the current. The older male nudged at them and growled once more.

It was no surprise to find what Lurveska most feared. An odd shape bobbed on the ripples amid a tinge of blood and foul metal. Approaching, she saw a hand with a stub of arm attached. The fingers were long, tipped with spiky claws, but the thumb was twisted inward, and the two middle fingers were joined by thick webbing.

Lurveska bit back a moan. Only Mizarit had that twisted thumb, those fingers weirdly bound together. The malformed limb was why the humans had brought the wailing infant here, more than a decade ago.

She had sensed the small group's intrusion at the edge of the swamp. Investigating, she watched from behind a screen of reeds as they roughly placed the babe on the bank without even a blanket to cover it.

"We can't just leave her," pleaded a woman. "The hags —!"

"Let them have her," their leader said. "This is how

our village will be saved from the curse."

The woman cried, until the leader raised a fist in threat. They went away then, with the mother still weeping. A tiny, twisted hand reached hopelessly after them. Lurveska had lingered, in case the humans changed their minds. While she waited, she plucked soft water weeds and knotted them into a coverlet. At last, she went to retrieve her child.

Humans passed many rumors among themselves, Lurveska knew. One of their favorites was about hags snatching children to be their supper. That was insulting, and ridiculous; it was far easier to catch fish in the swamp than to find a human child. Still, when the humans threw their children away, despising them for some minor deformity, the hags took them in. Hags were too much spirit and not enough animal to ever have children. However, through a succession of rituals, they could transform the youngsters into hags. Thus the guardianship of the Dolarus Swamp was assured.

Now Lurveska made ripples of her own, breathing hard as she gazed upon the severed hand of her hag-daughter. The limb had been cut off by a clean slash, well above the wrist. No beast could tear so sharply — even if they dared attack a hag. There was only one explanation.

"Humans." Sensing her mood, the younger water lizard plunged deep, away from her fury.

The thought of losing her hag-daughter was a terrible pain, like swallowing a fish with many bones. With a conscious effort, she slowed her angry breathing.

Lurveska was a hag, not some pitiful dry-lander who fell apart when things didn't go as they wished. A few forceful sweeps of her tail took her to the bottom, where she nipped off a lily pad and carried it back in her mouth. Shifting to hag form, she carefully wrapped Mizari's hand in the lily pad and tied it with the stem. In a section of wall where three columns leaned together, she tucked the parcel between the stones.

Later, if she must, there was a ritual to release Mizarit's spirit. For now, no part of her beloved daughter would be left to rot, unknown. And whoever had done this to her would face a reckoning.

Once more taking a lizard's form, Lurveska led her escort forward. More flotsam passed by, but no further trace of Mizarit. Lurveska tried to keep her focus.

In truth, she hardly needed the smoke to tell her where the invaders must be. Sele Daru always seemed to be the first place they tried to stake a claim. It was close to where a river flowed into the swamp. Humans were not fond of swimming, and the ruins of Sele Daru were slightly more intact, offering a suggestion of safety. There was even a circle of blackened stones, ready for a fire. For generations, her hag-mother Isanez had told her, hags would kill the intruders and scatter the stones. The next bunch would always build it again. Lurveska found the fire circle useful to lure them to that place, and so she left the stones where they were.

That may not have been wise. This time, she feared, it was Mizarit who had been lured.

128

When they were close enough, she chose a watching place. There was a section of wall with a pair of windows that gave a good view of the fire ring. In lizard form she crept from the water, then shifted back to herself and peered across the deceptively calm water.

There was the raddled paving, hidden in places by ages of reeds that had grown tall and died back. Vegetation had been trampled down to make space for a single tent near the fire ring. It was low and rounded, the cloth streaked with dull greens and browns to conceal it. Beside that was an upright post with a crossbar. The figure of an owl with up-standing ears had been carved at the top of it.

Fire burned in the circle, as expected. The damp fuel made for a sullen and smoky blaze. A small cauldron was propped over the flames. A single human strode back and forth around the fire.

"Just one?" Lurveska sneered to herself. He was a fool indeed, to dare the Dolarus Swamp alone. Yet she marked his clothing. No breeches and loose shirts, nor the broad hats favored by herder folk who hastily skirted past the ill-omened swamp. Instead, he wore long robes of shiny fabric, orange and red. His tasseled hat glinted with silver symbols. That explained one thing, at least. The human was a wizard.

On rare occasions, wizards from the Dry Lands would come to the Dolarus in search of certain herbs. Rarer still, a wizard asked politely to trade for these things, rather than making off with them. What little Lurveska knew of life in the Dry Lands came from speaking with them.

Based on what she had seen, this would not be a day for such conversation.

Yet, what she saw raised questions. Where were the swordsmen who had cut into the lizards? Who could she punish for maiming her daughter? Her connection with the creatures of the swamp didn't warn her of any other humans roaming around. Indeed, she sensed very few animals in the vicinity. Perhaps they had fled, or Mizarit had called on them for her ill-fated attack.

The wizard went on striding around the fire, bending frequently to collect objects that he piled up near the tent. Then, with visible effort, he lifted something else from the ground. Lurveska saw the shape of an arm, and a head sagging behind. So it was a body he moved? Mizarit must have fought well. Lurveska didn't let herself think about that battle's ending.

Cautiously, she reached out with her magic — and immediately recoiled. An unseen haze hung over Sele Daru. It felt much like the slick darkness that fouled the waters around Ava Zev. That was the evil of the Dolari, and no mistake!

This wizard could not be left to his own devices. There must be other creatures she could call upon. Snapping turtles grew to formidable size, but were slow to move on land. Some fishes grew large as well, but they couldn't leave the water. Only the biggest birds, eagles or cranes, would be able to reach her quickly enough.

While Lurveska stretched out her thoughts, the wizard returned to stir the cauldron. The carved figure stretched out jagged, leathery wings. Lurveska watched, startled. The creature was alive? She had thought it was a decoration. A piping voice floated across to her, something between an owl's screech and a bat's shrill pulse.

"Stop wasting time, fool! Get that potion done."

"I'm trying," the wizard snapped. He scattered something else into the cauldron and stirred vigorously. Sooty fumes billowed up. They gradually shifted to a nauseating yellow-gray.

So the wizard had a familiar, and Lurveska sensed that the source of its power was exactly the oily malevolence she knew from the waters around Ava Zev. Some poor owl had been snared by a restless demon, and twisted into this vicious little imp. The imp, in turn, had snared a human accomplice.

This was worse than treasure-hunting. The imp would have plans beyond what its companion imagined.

There was no time to wait for more help. Lurveska crouched to take on lizard form. As she slipped into the water, she directed her two lizards to circle around to the far side of Sele Daru. They dove deeper to swim unseen. She herself kept to the surface, moving slowly to maintain her stealth. The Dolari's miasma might blanket her magical awareness, but other senses still worked as well as ever.

It took a moment for her to smell something else besides the sour stench of the cauldron. Swampy and dank, but wholesome. Lurveska's heart jumped like a fish trying to snatch an insect from the air. Mizarit was there! Lurveska hadn't found any more remains because she wasn't dead. The wizard must have taken her prisoner.

Now that she knew, Lurveska sensed her hag daughter's mind clinging to sanity. Dolari malignance tried to smother her will, but she fought for her life. Stubborn, that was Mizarit. Oh beautiful, stubborn daughter! Lurveska reached back to her hag-daughter, trying to let her know that help was here.

It was a moment of weakness she immediately regretted. A shock of awareness flared between her and those intruders. Lurveska flinched away and floated at the surface, still as a bit of driftwood. The wizard stopped stirring the cauldron, and the imp on the post whipped around to stare over the water.

She could see them both well, now. The wizard had pale eyes and a pink face, sheened with sweat from the heat of his fire. Brown hair was pulled into a short tail behind the tasseled hat. He was plump, compared to a hag, but the silky robes hung off a gawky frame. In fact, the so-called wizard was hardly more than a boy.

"What was that?" He rubbed the back of his neck, uncertain.

This was addressed to the imp, a deceptively charming ball of gray fluff. Downy feathers covered its body, except for the leathery wings. It had round yellow eyes, a hooked beak, and small talons. What Lurveska had taken for feathered ears in fact were short horns. In place

132

of a feathered tail, a scorpion's sting curled beneath it.

"There's more than one hag, you fool," screeched the imp. "The first one is still fighting me. Get that potion into her."

"It's not ready," the wizard argued. "It's supposed to turn yellow and then green."

"We don't have time for perfection!"

"All right, all right." The wizard pulled back one sleeve and gingerly dipped a horn into the cauldron. Thick drops steamed down.

Whatever this potion was, Lurveska would not allow them to use it on her hag-daughter. Powerful tail sweeps drove her toward the bank. With a loud slosh, she shifted to hag form and rose abruptly from the murky water. The young wizard jumped. Dry reeds sizzled as his foul brew spattered down.

"There's another one!" The wizard yelled out the obvious.

Lurveska fixed them both with a baleful glare. "What do you think you're doing!"

Even as she spoke, a few details came out. The reeds were trampled down, splashed with dark stains. There was a second tent, now flattened. Near it lay two dead humans in leather and mail. Their weapons lay in a heap near the tent that was still standing. Some sort of emblem was embroidered on their tunics. It may have meant something in the Dry Lands, but here it was irrelevant.

The most important thing was Mizarit, chained down with bitter iron. Metal cuffs pinched her pearly gray skin and stained it black with poison. A stub of bone projected from her maimed stump. Blood tricked down, seeping into the mud. Mizarit did not seem to see Lurveska. Her lips curled back in a terrible, set grin, and liquid black eyes were fixed on nothing Lurveska could see.

"Fool," screeched the imp. "You took too long!"

Indignation flashed across the young wizard's face. He gathered himself and swaggered forward a little. "You are too late, hag. We beat this creature, and we'll beat you, too."

"Stop now," Lurveska commanded. Every moment she had to watch her daughter suffer was a spear stabbing into her gut, but she had to keep their eyes on her.

"Your foul magic has no power over us." The wizard bragged, but his voice was shrill and strained.

"If that is true, then why are you so afraid?" Lurveska prowled forward a little. The wizard shifted position to keep the boiling cauldron between them.

"We have come to reclaim the Chalice of All Waters, and you will not stop us!" His eyes darted, checking whether Mizarit had succumbed to the imp's will. The imp fluffed its feathers and gave a kind of malevolent chuckle. Its lurid golden gaze bore down on Mizarit. Her breath came in painful gusts, but she didn't whimper or cry out.

Lurveska told them, "The Chalice of All Waters is

cursed. It must remain here."

"That chalice is a sacred relic," ranted the young wizard. "You filthy hags stole it, and the Dry Lands have been crippled by centuries of drought. Did you think there would be no answer to your crimes?"

"The chalice was not stolen," Lurveska corrected sternly. "It was a gift, given freely and at great cost. Whoever told you so was lying."

She meant the imp, but the wizard bristled with indignation.

"Everyone knows the story of how it was stolen," he insisted. "Inorgarn, the Most Noble of Fallerad, gave us the task of fetching the chalice and saving his land from the drought."

"To save his little land, he would doom the world." Her tone held a bitter edge. "Yes, what a worthy deed for the Most Noble. I'm sure there was no prodding at all from that imp you cling to." Before he could reply, she swept out one long black claw to point at the miserable hag chained among the reeds. "And this? You dare to say we hags are evil."

Her chill fury made the wizard pale a little. Perhaps he actually felt guilt about what he was doing.

"She... That creature tried to stop us," he swaggered on. "We killed her beasts. Now she will be our guide in this accursed swamp. She will lead us to the forbidden palace of Ulu Anu, and we will take back our own."

"It will not happen," Lurveska vowed.

This was bad, that he knew the correct name of the chalice's resting place. Most humans only searched for baubles they had heard rumors of. Of course, most humans didn't have imps as their familiars.

"Get the potion, fool!" yelled the imp.

Again the wizard jumped, as one who was used to fearing the lash. Almost gratefully, he turned from Lurveska and rushed to bend over Mizarit. Lurveska's chest tightened with dread, but at last she saw two lizard heads cruising low in the water.

"Stop," she commanded, hoping to gain a little more time. "That is my daughter."

The wizard hesitated, steam rising from the horn. Lurveska could see the dismay in his eyes, a human response to her family appeal. His mouth opened and shut as if he couldn't decide what he should say. The imp, however, was delighted.

"Oh ho ho ho," it hooted with vicious triumph. "This is better than I hoped!"

"Give her back," Lurveska demanded, while the water lizards drifted stealthily closer.

"Gulgar," stuttered the young wizard, trying to reconcile this information with what he thought he knew about the dreaded hags of Dolarus Swamp. "Her daughter?"

"Don't turn weak now, boy," gloated the imp. "Step away, hag, and hear what I have to say."

The wizard still held the steaming horn, but he had stopped talking. Mizarit, too, seemed to lie a bit more easily. Black eyes glittered within her ashen face. Was it shame in those fevered eyes? A plea for help?

"There is nothing to talk about," Lurveska spat. The lizards had nearly reached the bank. "You will release her, and you will leave."

"Do you think your threats matter?" taunted the imp. "If you want this creature to go free, then it's very simple. I will release her if you agree to guide us to Ulu Anu."

"No," Mizarit croaked. "Don't." Then darksome power coiled around her, and she fell silent with a hiss.

Through her teeth, Lurveska vowed, "The chalice will remain in Ulu Anu. Leave while you can."

"What, no pity for your poor daughter?" mocked the imp. To the wizard, he commanded, "Get that potion."

"Do not," Lurveska warned.

The poor boy hesitated, looking first at his familiar and then at her. He must have glimpsed movement in the water, for his pale eyes widened and he opened his mouth to yell. Lurveska's call came faster.

"Now!"

The two water lizards lunged up the bank with guttural hisses and a wave of bog water. The wizard dropped the horn of potion and stumbled away, while the younger male made a leap at the imp. Hard jaws snapped just short of its target.

"You dare?" The imp shrieked, winging backward. Its scorpion tail lashed at the water lizard.

The wizard also scrambled back, pursued by the big old male, who outsized him both in length and bulk. One hand groped toward the heaped weapons, while the other began a series of passes through the air. The working was clumsy, but Lurveska felt his magic rising. Mizarit, meanwhile, gave a cry as she summoned her power. Imprisoned limbs shrank into short fins that no manacle could hold, and her body contracted into a streamlined trunk clad in silvery scales. A great gar fish now twisted and beat upon the bank.

Lurveska waited only long enough to see that her hag-daughter had escaped before she sprang into motion. Crouching, she shaped her arms into broad black wings, her legs into clawed talons. As a vulture, she flung herself into the air.

"This changes nothing!" The imp slashed with its sting. A ball of tarry light built between its talons. "The Dolari will not be denied. They will rise to glory again!"

"You are denied," Lurveska cried in a vulture's croak. "We hags will never be enslaved again!"

With vulture talons, she snatched at the much smaller imp. The vile creature jeered as it darted aside, but it had to let its working go. The ball of darkness winked out. Lurveska's broad wings gave her superior speed, and the sweep of her pinions swatted the imp toward the ground. Before it could right itself, the younger male jumped to catch it in his jaws. The imp's grating voice cut off as the water lizard slammed it against the paving stones once, twice, thrice.

Lurveska wheeled in the air. Still shaped as a gar, Mizarit arched and thrashed down the bank. She reached the water with a splash, and vanished from sight.

A few feet from there, the young wizard had managed to call flame to one of the dead warriors' blades. "Get away from me!" He struck out wildly at the older male lizard, which prowled, hissing, just beyond reach.

Moments later, her talons sank into his shoulders. The wizard yelled as they lurched into the air together. "No, I'm sorry," he babbled, kicking frantically. "Let me go. I didn't want to."

That was about the most stupid thing he could have said, but Lurveska reminded herself he had been deceived by the imp. Luckily, there was hardly any meat on the boy's bones.

"Hold still," she chided as his struggles unbalanced her.

He yelped and kept struggling. A flailing hand clutched her mussel-shell necklace. Despite that, Lurveska gained altitude. Strong wings swept them out across the pools and channels of the Dolarus Swamp. The boy let the necklace go and clung to her scaly legs. "I'm sorry," he babbled over and over.

"You are supposed to be a wizard," she scolded,

"someone who prizes knowledge. Look down and learn."

He went still at last, though with whimpers continuing to alternate between "let me go" and "don't drop me." It was hard to despise such a weakling, even if he deserved it.

"Just look," Lurveska commanded. "Search below the water. Tell me what you see."

She turned slowly, cupped her wings to keep them both steady. Below them, beyond his dangling feet and swirling robe, the murky skin of the water turned suddenly translucent. Everything below the surface sprang out. There were the sharp lines of drowned buildings, crossed here and there by sunken logs. Roofless courts spun beneath them, and dark stairways descended out of sight.

Among all this were the statues. They almost appeared to be outsized humans, until you saw their serpent tails, or bull heads, or horns and fangs, or vicious claws stretched toward the surface. Distorted faced gazed up, set with expressions of blood lust and cheated fury.

The young wizard jerked and gasped. Lurveska beat wings and asked, to be sure. "You see them?"

"Yes," he choked.

"They are why I will not let go," she rasped with cold mercy. "I will not feed those demons even one more drop of life."

Her prisoner was shivering. Lurveska's shoulders ached with the doubled weight, and her talons were

140

beginning to feel as if they might rip out of her toes. Gratefully, she glided back toward Sele Daru. With a vulture's sharp eyes, she scanned the paving and the water. Whatever else she had to say to this young fool, it could wait until she knew her hag-daughter was safe.

And — there! A hag emerged from the pool. Her garment of water weeds streamed water upon the bank. The two water lizards circled around, greeting her. As Lurveska descended, she saw a dark spatter across the stones. The lizards had tracked the imp's blood around, but there was no sign of the imp itself.

Relieved beyond words, Lurveska dropped to the pavement. Her trembling passenger tottered away with frantic haste. She shifted back to her natural form and ran to embrace Mizarit. There was the stick-thin frame, water weeds and lank hair dripping against her own.

"You're safe," she cried. "Besides the hand, did he hurt you?"

"Of course I'm safe," Mizarit answered indignantly. "You trained me. And, Mother, look!" She pulled away and held up her hands. Not one hand and a stump — two hands! If one of them had a twisted thumb and fingers bound in a web of flesh, that hardly seemed to matter. "I shifted to escape the chains, and when I changed back, I had two hands again."

"Because the image of yourself, in your mind, has two hands." Lurveska's knees felt a little odd, probably because she would not have to hold any rituals over her hag-daughter's death. "Well done, my daughter."

Mizarit nodded gratefully, but her eyes narrowed when she turned toward the wizard. He had retrieved the same blade as before, but not set it afire. The old water lizard had taken up a position near him. Beady eyes glinted with grim focus.

"I took care of the others," Mizarit said proudly, "but what about this one?"

The wizard shied away, but then straightened. Belatedly, he tried to shake his robes into order. The satin folds were no longer so fine. Streaks and stains marred their sheen. Spots of blood, too. A moment stretched among them. Much as Lurveska approved of Mizarit's strength of will, to stay and confront the one who had wounded her, this would not be as simple as she seemed to think.

"I didn't know," the boy stuttered. Lurveska watched carefully for any sign that he would rally a new attack, but the pale eyes only darted anxiously between them.

"Yes, you did." Mizarit gave a curt laugh. "Why would you even come here, if you didn't know?"

"Patience," Lurveska said. Coolly, she studied the young wizard. Most humans were afraid of hags, or all too ready for battle. This one, at least, had hesitated even against the goading of his familiar. "Well, what shall we do with you?"

There was a flicker of hope in his expression, that he would not die right away. Stiffly, he said, "I apologize."

Mizarit folded her arms, disgust written across her

thin face. "You aren't really a wizard, are you?" she accused. "That imp did all the work."

"That's not true," he complained.

"He conjured flame to his blade. That is not nothing," Lurveska said. Mizarit huffed indignantly. "The emergency is over, so let us take stock."

The human broke in, "I am a wizard. Or... I could be." Under Lurveska's bland gaze, he rushed on. "There have been times. Unexplained events, when I was very angry or afraid. Gulgar said I could achieve great things, if I let him teach me."

"Great things," Mizarit sniffed.

"He taught you that which made you a useful pawn," Lurveska said. "You do understand that? His purpose was to destroy the Chalice and set the Dolari free."

Shamefaced, he nodded, but then blurted, "He didn't tell me that."

"Didn't tell you," Mizarit mock-whined.

"I said that I apologize!"

Mizarit would have retorted, but Lurveska raised a hand. "Daughter, stop. I believe it is possible to salvage something from this, and an apology is not a bad place to begin." They both regarded her, the young wizard startled and the young hag indignant. "What name shall we call you, human?"

"Raevon."

"How did you come to have such a familiar, Raevon?" Lurveska was aware of Mizarit drawing angry claws through the long strands of her hair, but for now she held her peace.

"He was just in the barn one day. In the rafters." Raevon gave an uneasy shrug. "He said that he knew I needed him."

"He wasn't wrong," Lurveska admitted. "You do have power in that potion."

"That was the imp," Mizarit argued.

"No," he insisted, pink face darkening. "He told me what to do, but I made that."

"Don't brag about it," Mizarit sniffed. "I don't even know what that gunk would have done to me."

The two young people glared at each other, equally stubborn. Lurveska smiled, relieved only that her hag-daughter was alive to be so obstinate.

"Well, so," she intervened. "Did you truly go to the Most Noble Inorgarn, offering Gulgar's plan to lift the drought from the Dry Lands?"

"The Most Noble was doubtful, but he did provide retainers." Raevon stuttered a little, remembering that those retainers were dead, then rushed on. "He will know if we do not return."

"Don't threaten us," Mizarit flared.

"That was not my thinking," Lurveska replied. "If I give you a message for the Most Noble, will he believe that it does come from the Dolarus Swamp?"

"I think so." Raevon looked slightly less anxious.

"Then, this is the message," Lurveska said. "The Dolari are real. Long ago, they held both humans and spirits in bondage. Our ancestors were not enemies, but allies who created the Chalice of All Waters together. It was never stolen. Its waters are enchanted to endlessly smother the power of the Dolari."

"All right, but when so much water is taken into the Dolarus Swamp, all the rest of the world goes dry," he objected. "Nobody can live."

"The Chalice is powerful, but the water has to come from somewhere," Lurveska acknowledged. "Yet if the Dolari ever return, nobody will be living then, either."

"Besides, it's been centuries. There are still enough humans to come hunting treasure in the swamp," Mizarit added. "We hags have to keep fighting you off."

"Just so," Lurveska agreed. "Here is my offer — return to the Most Noble. Tell him my message. Once, we spirits of this world were allied with humans. We could be again."

Lurveska could guess what Raevon was thinking from his downcast expression. The imp must have promised the Most Noble gold and glory, thriving farms and well-fed people, all based on more water than his kingdom could ever want. Those dreams were now sinking into the mire of Dolarus Swamp.

"He won't like that,"Raevon worried. However,

what the Most Noble liked or disliked was not Lurveska's concern.

"It cannot be helped, and remember this — everything those demons touched became cursed. The Chalice of All Waters, the Sword of Char Chish, the Tome of Nin Kye. They all are cursed."

Raevon stirred restlessly. Lurveska went on, sternly.

"Consider: even if the Kingdom of Fallerad had the chalice, the rest of the world would still be dry. Don't you think they might try to seize such a prize for themselves? Fallerad would never know peace again."

"Oh," he mumbled. Mizarit smirked.

"As to yourself," Lurveska went on. "An untrained wizard is a danger to all. Was there any other wizard among the court of the Most Noble who could teach you honest magic?"

"I don't know," Raevon faltered. "Maybe, but they were so jealous of Gulgar that I hardly knew them."

"Jealous," Mizarit challenged, "or did they know better than to take up with an imp?"

Raevon scowled, and Lurveska scolded her daughter with a glance. Then to the young wizard, she said, "Go to them. Ask to be trained in wholesome ways. If they will not, then return to me. I may know of one or two human wizards who understand what's at stake."

"What? I don't want him back here," Mizarit complained.

"I only said if the other wizards won't help," Lurveska countered, "and must you keep interrupting?"

Now it was Raevon who smirked at Mizarit's pout. "I'll try," he said.

The young human looked around uncertainly, hemmed in by the two water lizards of Lurveska's escort. At her nod, the big old one moved back. Raevon scurried to snatch up a few belongings and was soon jumping from hummock to hummock, headed back to the edge of the swamp. The two water lizards followed at a distance, making certain he didn't turn aside.

Mizarit watched as he left. Restless fingers rubbed the hand that had been cut off. On the bank nearby, Lurveska murmured, "I should have been here, instead of you."

"Why? I did what I could," Mizarit snapped, as defensive as the young wizard Raevon. "You shouldn't have let him go. He might not even go to this 'Most Noble.' What if he comes back with more soldiers?"

"Having lost two, the Most Noble is unlikely to waste more," Lurveska reasoned. "Besides, the young man seems to have learned something."

"We're supposed to protect the swamp. Those humans can't be allowed to come and go," Mizarit protested.

"I did protect the swamp," Lurveska answered. "The imp was the true threat. It no longer is. Besides, if we are able to form an alliance, that is also a way to protect the swamp."

"That's just wishful thinking," Mizarit said.

"Magic is wishful thinking made real. Isn't that what we hags are?" Lurveska retorted. No matter how stubborn Mizarit was, she couldn't feel anything but joy that her hag-daughter had survived her first invasion. "Besides, there is more than one way to fight. When you are the only hag in the Dolarus Swamp, you will understand."

Mizarit nodded, but she discontentedly kicked at one of the humans' wooden shields. After a moment longer, Lurveska joined her.

"You're right, let's clear this off."

Together, the two hags dragged weapons, corpses, and other bits of debris into the nearest pool. Tent fabric billowed, fighting the water, until Mizarit tossed a broken pole into the midst of it. The campfire still smoldered and flared. A wave of Lurveska's hand brought silty water to drown the flames. The potion would have to cool before she dumped it into the swamp, and she hoped it wouldn't poison anything. Those cursed stones of the fire ring would have to be disposed of as well.

Later, Lurveska would want to hear more details about how her hag-daughter had fought the humans, and how many animals the swamp had lost. For now, it was enough to know Mizarit was alive, and so was the possible alliance.

Humans and hags had been allies, long ago. Perhaps they would be again.

Aunt Anne's Archive

About the Author

Deby Fredericks has been a writer all her life, but thought of it as just a fun hobby until the late Nineties. Since then she has published twenty fantasy novels, novellas and novelettes, either with small presses or independently. Her short fiction has appeared in *Andromeda Spaceways,* selected anthologies, and small magazines.

Since 2018, her significant work has been the *Minstrels of Skaythe* series, about a group of pacificist mages who seek hope in a world ruled by darkness.

In addition, Fredericks writes for children as Lucy D. Ford. Her children's stories and poems have appeared in magazines such as *Boys' Life, Babybug, Ladybug*, and *Spider.* In the past, she served as Regional Advisor for the Inland Northwest Region of the Society of Children's Book Writers and Illustrators, International (SCBWI).

But wait, there's more! Fredericks has been involved with science fiction fandom in Eastern Washington since the early Eighties. She worked on the convention committees of Spokon, InCon, WesterCon 49 and SpoCon. In addition to her leadership of Telgar Weyr (Pern fandom), she was involved with Star Trek and Elfquest fan groups, and a few independent comic projects. Fredericks was the Fan Guest of Honor at RadCon 1, RustyCon 21, was Author Guest of Honor at RadCon 9, and has been a frequent panelist at Inland Northwest conventions.

To Find Out More

Learn more from her web site, www.debyfredericks.com or her blog, wyrmflight.wordpress.com

www.ingramcontent.com/pod-product-compliance
Lightning Source LLC
Chambersburg PA
CBHW060227180626
46813CB00007B/2984